The Meanest Hound Around

BOOKS BY BILL WALLACE

Aloha Summer
The Backward Bird Dog
Beauty
The Biggest Klutz in Fifth Grade
Blackwater Swamp
Buffalo Gal
The Christmas Spurs
Coyote Autumn
Danger in Quicksand Swamp
Danger on Panther Peak
[Original title: Shadow on the Snow]
A Dog Called Kitty
Eye of the Great Bear
Ferret in the Bedroom, Lizards in the Fridge
The Final Freedom
Goosed!
Journey into Terror
Never Say Quit
Red Dog
Skinny Dipping at Monster Lake
Snot Stew
Totally Disgusting!
Trapped in Death Cave
True Friends
Upchuck and the Rotten Willy
Upchuck and the Rotten Willy: The Great Escape
Upchuck and the Rotten Willy: Running Wild
Watchdog and the Coyotes

BOOKS BY CAROL AND BILL WALLACE

The Flying Flea, Callie, and Me
That Furball Puppy and Me
Chomps, Flea, and Gray Cat (That's Me!)
Bub Moose
Bub, Snow, and the Burly Bear Scare
The Meanest Hound Around

BOOKS BY NIKKI WALLACE

Stubby and the Puppy Pack
Stubby and the Puppy Pack to the Rescue

Available from Simon & Schuster

The Meanest Hound Around

Carol Wallace
and
Bill Wallace

Illustrated by
John Steven Gurney

ALADDIN PAPERBACKS
New York London Toronto Sydney

First Aladdin Paperbacks edition July 2004

Text copyright © 2003 by Carol Wallace and Bill Wallace
Illustrations copyright © 2003 by John Steven Gurney

ALADDIN PAPERBACKS
An imprint of Simon & Schuster
Children's Publishing Division
1230 Avenue of the Americas
New York, NY 10020

Also available in a Simon & Schuster Books for
Young Readers hardcover edition.

Printed in the United States of America
2 4 6 8 10 9 7 5 3

The Library of Congress has cataloged the
hardcover edition as follows:
Wallace, Carol, 1948-
The meanest hound around / by Carol Wallace and Bill Wallace ;
illustrated by John Steven Gurney.
p. cm.
Summary: After being abandoned, Freddie helps a mild-tempered
dog named Spike escape from a cruel junkyard owner and the two
manage to survive on their own until they find a loving home.
ISBN 0-7434-3785-3 (hc.)
[1. Dogs—Fiction.]
I. Wallace, Bill. II. Gurney, John, ill. III. Title.
PZ7.W15475 Me 2003
[Fic.]—dc21
2002152821
ISBN 0-7434-3786-1 (pbk.)

To
Marian Staton
and
Jennifer Brock

The Meanest
Hound Around

CHAPTER 1

Wet. I never felt so wet. I was soaked. Trying to make myself smaller, I hunched my shoulders and leaned to the right. A rivulet of water streamed down from the big limb above my head. The drops hit smack-dab between my shoulder blades.

Leaning to the left, I got away from that stream, but more water leaked from a knot on the other side of the limb. It hit right between my ears, trickled down to the tip of my snout, and dripped off my whiskers.

Beneath this huge tree was the driest spot I had found. Even so, I was still drenched—soaked clear to the skin. Water even dripped from my tummy, adding to the puddle at my feet.

I couldn't understand. My boy would never leave me out here . . . not all night . . . not all alone. . . .

We played chase in the backyard. He petted me and hugged me. I licked his face and ears and he laughed. I loved him. He loved me. My boy would never desert me.

Just then a big drop of rain hit right inside my ear. I flinched and shook my head.

It wasn't my boy. It was the daddy. He was the one who brought me here.

The day had started out okay. My boy fed me, petted me, and we'd had a little romp. When my boy left for school, the daddy put me on my leash and we went for a drive in the car. I should have known then, because there was something different about the way he acted. Something strange and unusual. Besides that, my boy wasn't with us. He was always there when we went for a ride.

I sat in the backseat and watched the road. Things didn't look familiar when we stopped. The daddy took my collar off and let me run. But when I came back to the car . . . the car was gone. Maybe I romped and played too long. Maybe I didn't come back when I should have. I don't know.

Anyway, I sat and waited and waited and waited. I just knew he wouldn't leave me.

The first night was really bad. When I was little I'd slept in a big basket with my mother and brothers and sisters. When my boy took me to live with him, I had to sleep outside. I had my own doghouse, though, and there was a big fence to keep all the nighttime scaries from getting too close. Out here, I was all alone with no place to hide. Then it got worse. It started to rain. Two days and one night the rain fell. Still I waited. I just knew they would come for me. Cold, miserable, scared, and lonely, I waited. Now . . . I'd waited long enough. It was time to move on.

Someone growled at me. It snapped me from my thoughts and made me jump. The growl came again, but this time I realized that it wasn't someone growling at me . . . it was my tummy.

With a heavy heart (not to mention my heavy wet fur) I knew it was time to go. I couldn't wait any longer.

As I walked I looked for anything familiar. When the rain finally stopped, I didn't. I kept walking. Never slowing down, I sniffed for those special scents of home. They weren't there.

What I did smell was kind of interesting, though. It was like the car and the trash and metal and . . . well, it reeked of everything all jumbled together. I followed the aroma to a big chain-link fence. It was like the one in my backyard, only taller. The top had wire wrapped around it. I had never seen anything quite like it. There was stuff piled everywhere. My nose wiggled as I whiffed along the edge of the fence. With all that junk and trash, there had to be *something* in there to eat.

"Get away from here, you mangy mutt!" a short black dog snarled at me. "This is my yard. Get on your way. I have work to do."

"Chill, mister, I'm just looking. Besides I don't know how to get in there anyway." I stared at the white teeth that shined back at me.

"I'm serious. You'd better get away from here. I mean it!" The dog's ears flattened against his head and his eyes narrowed. At the same time, though, his tail was wagging. He stuck his nose through one of the chain-link squares.

My tail started wagging, too. I leaned down and licked his nose with my pink tongue.

"Hey, stop that!" His light brown eyebrows crooked as he stepped back and growled again. The fur on his neck stood out to make him look bigger.

I dropped my head to stare him in the eye. "You need to calm down. You're going to wear out the fur on your neck."

"Get real! If I let you hang around, the junk-yard guy will kick me. I've got work to do." The dog stepped back up to the fence and sniffed at me.

I licked his face again. "Hey, what's your name, anyway?" I asked.

"Which name do you want?"

"You have more than one name? How did that happen?"

"Well, these guys call me Spike. But my first name was April."

My nose twitched and my ears perked up. "April? That's a funny name for a *boy* dog."

"Yeah, maybe, but I kind of like it. This little kid gave me that name. She was pretty sweet to me. She was a bit rough, I guess, but nothing compared to Roy. He is just mean!" The dog sat down on his haunches and relaxed.

"What should I call you?" I twitched my ears at him.

"Better call me Spike. If Tiger hears anyone call me April, I'll be in more trouble than ever." He stretched out, crossed his front legs, then dropped his head to rest on his paws.

"Who's Tiger?" I asked.

"Tiger is the Junkyard Dog. He is *really* mean. Roy has been poking him with a stick and kicking him forever. So he got his attitude adjusted a long time ago. Roy is working on me, but I'm not mean yet. He says that I'll get there, though." Spike scooted on the ground until his nose touched the fence. "By the way, what's your name?"

"Freddie. Call me Freddie." I closed my eyes. . . .

* * *

The boy had picked me special. I was the third one to leave the litter. He had looked me all over and declared, "You are Fred D. Fluff Dog! I will love you forever."

That was before the car ride. The ride that got me here . . . the junkyard. . . .

"Just call me Freddie." I sighed. "That's what my friends call me. Just Freddie." My ears drooped. My stomach grumbled.

From the back of the yard a big yellow dog came running at us.

"Spike, what are you doing? Run that white pile of fluff away from here. You aren't doing your job. Get busy! Get rid of that mutt!" I could see the dog's huge muscles under his short golden hair. Black stripes stretched across his chest and back.

Spike sprang to his feet and spun to face him. "I . . . er, I . . . ah . . . thought that was only people that we had to keep away," he stammered. "This is just a dog!"

My new friend looked sort of small and helpless as he stood next to the other dog.

"What are you thinking? One more dog

around here, and we won't get anything to eat. We barely get enough as it is. Get rid of him. Now!" Tiger snapped his strong jaws at Spike's ear.

"Get out of here, you big fluff ball," Spike growled at me. Then he winked. "Go around the corner and wait," he whispered softly so Tiger couldn't hear.

I looked into his narrowed eyes, flipped my tail, and ran out of sight. Hiding behind some wooden boxes, I waited for some kind of signal. It wasn't long before I heard a friendly yip.

Carefully peeking around the edge of the boxes, I kept my ears low in case Tiger was still there. Spike stood next to the fence.

"It's okay," he said with a wag of his tail. "Tiger has gone on patrol. I'm supposed to keep you away. Just make sure that you watch out for him. It takes quite awhile for Tiger to get all the way around the whole yard. What are you doing here, anyway? You look like somebody has been taking care of you." Spike stretched out and touched his nose against the fence.

I shrugged my ears. "I got dumped. I think."

Spike arched an eyebrow. "What happened?"

"I don't know. I thought the daddy was taking me for a car ride. I got out for a run, and when I came back . . ." My head drooped when I thought about it.

"Yeah, you got dumped, all right! It happens to the best of us. Things are going along just dandy, and the next thing you know . . . dumped!" Spike jumped up and started biting at his rear end. "Pesky fleas!"

"I didn't do anything. My boy and I were happy together. He loved me. I am sure of it." My heart raced as I remembered the feeling I had when the car didn't come back for me.

"You didn't *have* to do anything! Stuff just happens. Something went wrong with them. Your boy probably still loves you. It's his parents with the problem. Who knows. You gotta live for the day." Spike reached up to scratch his belly with his hind leg.

"I don't know." I sighed. "Maybe if I had minded them better. I got along great with my boy. Maybe I dug too many holes in the yard. Maybe I barked too much." I sagged to the ground and rested my nose against the fence.

"Yeah, maybe, but quit worrying about it. People are just like that. Sometimes there's no reason at all. *You can't trust people.* At least you are free. Look at the mess I'm in. You are the first dog that I have had a chance to talk to. Tiger won't even play chase with me. Well, he does, but he bites me if he catches me—really hard. If you think you have it bad, you need to be in my yard for a while."

"How could it be worse?" I sighed. "One day I have a warm house in a nice safe yard. A boy and toys to play with. Then . . . I get dumped."

Spike gave a snort. It was so loud it almost sounded like a growl. "You think you got it bad? Well, just let me tell you about bad. . . ."

CHAPTER 2

"My life started out pretty good, I guess." Spike's ears perked up when he glanced over his shoulder. "Be sure you watch out for Tiger behind me."

"Okay." I nodded.

"My ma was super," he went on. "I only had two sisters and two brothers, so we had lots of time to play and plenty to eat. It was great. My first home was a really nice doghouse. It was close to the people. They watched us and kept us safe from coyotes and dangerous stuff out in the woods. There were two little kids there. They played with us all the time. They even took us for walks. When we got tired, one of them would pick us up and snuggle up close." Spike stretched out on his belly with his front paws crossed.

"How did you end up here?" I asked.

"That's a good question. We dug in the yard, we chased butterflies, we barked at cars that came up to the house. Things were great. Our people started giving us dog food, mixed with milk. One day Ma started getting cranky with us. She snarled at us when we got too close to her. I don't know what happened." Spike snapped his head around and chewed at his side.

"I think she was trying to wean you. It was time for you to be on your own." I flopped down on my stomach, still keeping my nose against the fence.

"Yeah, I guess. Anyhow it wasn't long before Roy came to the house and picked up my sister Joy and me. I don't know what happened to her. I fell asleep in the car. When I woke up, I was stuck in a little cage. Roy kept me there for a long time. He barely fed me and he didn't keep my cage clean. It was awful." Spike jumped up, chased his tail, then tumbled onto his back and rolled in the rocks. He started chewing at the fleas again.

"That doesn't sound too good, but at least you didn't get dumped!" I stood up and shook my fur. Watching Spike bite at his fleas made me itch all over.

"Hang on, it gets worse. While I was stuck in the little cage, Tiger would come by and growl and snap at me. Ma was cranky, but nothing compared to Tiger. Every time he patrolled the yard, he made sure that he stuck his big ugly face up to my cage. Then there was Roy."

"What did Roy do?"

"At first he just stuck a stick in the cage and jabbed me. I pushed myself as far from him as possible, but I just couldn't get away. I didn't growl or bark or anything. So he got some kind of thing that stung me. I started snarling when that happened. Roy would laugh and do it again. It was terrible. He didn't let me out of that little cage until I was almost too big for it." Spike suddenly jumped to all four feet. He perked his ears and looked all around.

"Did you hear Tiger?"

He shook his head. "Guess it was just my imagination."

"Was it better after you got out of the cage?" I stared at him.

"Sort of." He stopped again and tilted his head to one side. "Do you hear anything? We don't want Tiger or Roy to catch us."

I sat up and perked my ears. "I don't hear a sound."

"Yeah, things did get a little bit better. I could hide sometimes, but mostly I had to be on patrol. If Roy caught me asleep, he'd poke me with the sting stick. If I growled, he left me alone. If not, I got jabbed again. It's been like that for a long time." Spike shook the dust off.

"Well, he feeds you, doesn't he? I haven't eaten in two days. Do you have anything that you can share with me?"

"Yeah, he feeds us. He even has our bowls in different places so that Tiger can't get all my food. It's almost time to eat, I think. Follow me. I'll show you where my bowl is. I'll share some with you. Come on." Spike trotted away from the fence and disappeared behind some car parts.

I squinted my eyes to see where he went. There were piles of junk on the outside of the fence, as well as on the inside. Moving around the clutter, I kept watch. Tiger didn't scare me, 'cause I was outside the fence. But I didn't want Spike to get in trouble. Roy was something else. If nice people dumped good dogs like me, and Roy poked sweet dogs like Spike with a sting stick . . . I had to be careful.

I strolled behind a stack of wood, then around some old metal barrels. When I got back to the fence I could see Spike's doghouse on the other side. It was wood with cracks between the boards where cold rain and wind could whistle through. His empty bowl leaned against his house.

"It won't be too long before Roy or Zack brings some food." Spike flipped his head around. "You'll have to hide when they come up."

"Who's Zack?"

"Zack works here sometimes. He isn't mean like Roy, but he has to act like he is or Roy gets mad." Spike shoved a toenail of his hind foot into his ear and scratched another flea.

"What time do they feed you? I'm starving."

"I think I hear him now. You've got to hide.

Go back by those bushes until he leaves."

As soon as I started off, Spike hopped to his feet. Tail wagging, he spun around to go greet a short, skinny man with a bald head.

As soon as I got to the bushes, I flattened out and tried to hide in the dirt.

"Hey, Spike! How's it going?" When the man smiled his greeting, he looked kind of funny. All his teeth were crooked and there was a big, black, empty space where one of his front teeth should have been. Still, he seemed nice. "You doing your job today?" the man asked as he poured dry dog food into Spike's bowl. Cautious . . . almost nervous, he glanced all around as if to make sure no one was watching. Then he dropped down and rubbed Spike's ears. "Gotta go! Be a mean dog."

I lay perfectly still until the man was gone.

"Hey, Freddie. Come and get it!" Spike shoved the bowl with his nose until it was almost to the fence.

Taking one last look all around, I raced to him.

"Sorry." He sighed. "But this is the best I can do." Quick as he could, Spike began shoveling dog food through the fence with his snout.

I ate a few of the pieces. They were hard, but just the sound of food crunching made my tummy feel better. Spike nibbled at his meal.

Suddenly his ears shot up, and he jerked his head around.

"Look out! Here comes Tiger!"

I spun and ran for some barrels.

"Grrr—get out of here you mangy dog! I've already warned you to stay away." Spike growled low in his throat.

"Did you let that dirty ball of fur come back here?" Tiger snarled at Spike, then jumped at the fence with his front paws. His lips curled back and his teeth looked wet and shiny.

I ducked behind one of the barrels, waited a second, then peeked around it. Tiger was snarling and biting at Spike.

"You trying to get us in trouble? Don't let that shabby canine near here. Roy's coming and he's going to be mad. You know better than to let some strange dog near the place."

Tiger towered over Spike. All I could do was watch as he snapped and growled at my new friend.

"What are you two filthy beasts doing out here?" Suddenly another man was standing over the dogs kicking at both of them. He poked them with a tree branch.

"Grrr . . . Leave me alone!" Tiger stood tall and straight as he growled back.

"Shut up, you nasty scoundrel. I'm in charge here." Roy kicked him in the side.

Tiger let out a little yelp and backed away. Spike ran to hide behind a pile of wood. I flattened myself against the ground as I watched the scene in front of me.

The man chased after Tiger and grabbed him by the neck, shoving him to the ground. The vicious dog snarled and growled, but he didn't bite the man.

"Shut up before I throw your ugly tail in a cage. You're supposed to be keeping robbers out of my junkyard, not fighting with the other dog. Go on, get!" Roy turned and stomped away.

Tiger started licking his side where the man had kicked him. Spike's head hung low as he cowered back toward his bowl to finish his meal. For no reason and with no warning, Tiger tore into him.

Teeth bared, he slashed and snapped at the smaller dog. Spike fell to the ground and tried to protect his throat.

"This is all your fault. Keep that dog away from here. If I catch you being nice to him again, I'll chew you up for good." Tiger swaggered away.

Spike was right. This *was* worse than being dumped. I had found a friend, but he lived in constant terror of being attacked by Tiger or Roy, and there was nothing I could do to help him.

CHAPTER 3

I watched until Tiger was completely out of view. Then I waited some more. I finally crawled closer to the fence. My back feet dragged along as I pulled with my front paws. I kept as low to the ground as I could.

"Why don't you run away?" I asked, pressing my nose against the fence.

"How am I going to get out? They keep the gate locked even when they're here. Roy or Zack checks the fence every day to make sure there are no new holes under the chain link." Spike's tongue rubbed at the wounds on his side. His ears drooped where Tiger had chewed at them.

"There has to be a way out. Have you looked

at the whole fence?" I jumped to my feet and started to walk along the pen.

"Don't be silly," Spike scoffed. "They check and guard it all the time. You don't want to run into Roy anywhere. If you really have to look for yourself, you'd better wait until he goes home. Tiger can't get through the fence to get you, but he will let Roy or Zack know that you are out there. They'll come after you for sure. You're a lot better off right where you are." Spike started licking his front legs.

"When do they leave? I'll start looking as soon as they are gone." I perked my ears.

"You'll have to wait until it's almost dark," he answered. "Roy brings Zack here in that old truck that's parked by the front gate. It makes so much noise that you can hear them when they leave. Just keep your ears perked. You can't miss it."

"I know there has to be some way out of this big cage." I looked one way, then the other. "Maybe you could sneak out under their feet when they leave."

"I don't think so. I tried that once. They tied me up for two days. Don't really want to do that again. I'm pretty tired right now." Spike groaned as he curled to one side.

"Don't worry, Spike. We'll figure a way out of this. There has to be something we can do to get you to safety."

"You're a pretty positive kind of dog for one that was dumped just this week. Get real. I'm trapped in and you're trapped out—neither one of us is living the good life. You'd better just hit the road as soon as they are gone. Don't look back. If you're lucky, somebody may take you in. You're a good-looking dog, somebody may want you. Just don't let it be Roy." Spike scrunched into a ball.

It seemed like forever before I finally heard the roar of the truck's engine. Spike barely twitched his ears.

I scampered to my feet. I didn't want to alert Tiger. Roy was gone, and the big, nasty bully could bark his head off, but no one would hear him. Tiger couldn't get out of the pen to get me, but he *could* hurt my friend.

I hadn't moved very far when Tiger strolled around the corner. He stood over Spike and snarled, "Get up, you worthless mangy dog. It's worktime, not naptime."

"I'm up. I'm going." Spike cautiously pulled himself to his feet. His legs trembled as he watched the ridge on Tiger's back bristle.

"You'd better do a good job. If it wasn't for me, they would have run you off a long time ago. I have to do my work and yours. Now go on. And keep that big white dog from coming back." Tiger towered over the frightened pup as he snorted his commands. "I heard you talking to him. Roy will try to turn him into a watchdog, and then there sure won't be enough to eat. Get moving!"

"I'm going. I'm going. I'll get my job done." Spike eased away from Tiger slowly. Tiger's legs were stiff and straight. His shoulders firm and rigid.

I crouched lower. I wanted to disappear into the ground. Tiger stared as Spike moved out of sight. Finally he kicked the dirt with his hind legs, turned, and walked the opposite way.

When my muscles finally relaxed, I crept along the fence, following in the direction that Spike had gone. When I spotted him, he was sitting near a pile of wood, scratching.

"Yip, yip. Spike, over here. Come here," I yelped softly to him.

"Are you still here? I thought you would have been long gone by now. Didn't you see what Tiger did to me? You'd better get on your way."

"No, I'm not leaving you. You're my friend. We're going to get you out of here somehow. We just need a plan, and I think I've got one. Keep patrolling. The next time you come this way, stop and I'll let you know what it is." I scooted away from the fence.

"Are you sure? This seems pretty hopeless to me. After a while you get kind of used to it."

"No, really. We can do it," I assured him. "I'm going to get you out. Just give me a few minutes. I think you're too short to jump over the fence, but there has to be a way."

"You really think so? I've been wanting to get out of here for a long time, but it hasn't happened yet. Like I said, I tried to get through the gate once and ended up tied with a chain. That was awful. You'd better go on. Save yourself!" Spike stared at me.

"We can do it. I just need some time to think." I licked the whiskers on the right side of my mouth, then nibbled at my bottom lip. I just had to come up with a plan. . . .

"Okay. I'll make a patrol. Will you be here?" Dust flew in the twilight as Spike shook himself.

I nodded my head so hard that my ears flopped.

"I'll be here."

I touched the fence and waited for Spike to get close enough to lick him with my tongue.

"I believe you will come up with a plan. Make sure you don't let Tiger see you. I'll be in big trouble if he knows you're still here." Spike licked at the fence.

I stayed hidden until Tiger finally patrolled back around. As soon as he was gone, I leaped up and ran to the fence. My plan would work. Digging. I was an excellent digger. I had dug out of my yard before. I had dug up the flowers at my old house. The gophers were always asking me to dig for them. This would work.

* * *

By the time Spike came by, I had a pile of dirt next to the fence. I was making progress.

"Hey, Freddie, what are you doing? Are you crazy? Tiger will see that pile so quick." Mouth gaping wide, Spike stared at the brown mound.

"No, that's where the plan comes in. You have to do your part, though." I snorted, to blow some of the dust from my nose.

Spike's tail tucked. "I'm telling you, Tiger's going to see that."

"That's where you come in. When he gets here, you're going to go running to him. Get him to go with you to the other side of the junkyard."

"How?"

"I don't know. Tell him that you heard something, or that something ran by. That way he won't have time to check this place out. It'll work. It's a good plan. I'll dig this whole part. When I finish, I'll go to the far side of the junkyard and yip at him or something. Then you start working on your side. He'll be so busy barking at me that you can get out. It'll work!" I grinned at him and wagged my tail.

"Sounds like a super plan, Freddie. Just one little thing."

"Yeah, it's great, isn't it? We've got to get busy! Go on patrol some more," I encouraged.

"No, you don't get it. I don't know how to dig!" Spike's jowls drooped.

My mouth flew open, and I blinked about three times.

"Can't dig? You're a dog. All dogs can dig."

"Not me. I tried. It doesn't work."

"Anybody can dig. You just put your paws out and burrow into the ground. You can do it." I looked him in the eye.

"I *can't* dig." Spike's head sagged low to the ground.

"You can do it. Gophers can dig. Even stupid cats can dig. Just put your paw out, and things will happen naturally." I stuck out my paw and started digging.

Spike moved closer to the fence. His eyes pierced into the dusk.

"Come on, get busy. We don't have time to mess around." I looked up briefly to see what Spike was doing.

It seemed like forever, but he finally tapped at the ground with his paw.

"You've got to put some backbone into it. Shove down with your claws, then pull back like you're going to get a sticker out. The topsoil may be hard, but it gets easier as you get farther down." I kept digging, but I watched from the corner of my eye.

Spike patted at the ground until he finally got some dirt out with one claw.

"I've got it! Look. We *can* do it." Spike's hind legs jumped around like crazy.

"Well, not quite, but it's a good try. Look, Spike, go take Tiger over to the other side. As soon as you can get away from him, hurry back here. I'll keep working. I think you can get the hang of it, but we don't want to get caught." I sniffed at him.

I dug and dug. Maybe this would be harder than I thought. I'd have to dig all of my side, then scoop under the fence as much as I could. Spike needed a lot of encouragement with his digging.

The opening under the fence was almost wide enough when Spike trotted back to me.

"Tiger is howling at some coyotes right now. He fell for that pretty easily. The coyotes helped. They were already yapping at a train whistle." Spike dropped his nose closer to the hole.

More dirt flew between my hind legs. "Get busy, Spike. We only have a little time. The coyotes won't keep him busy forever."

Spike sniffed the spot that he had started. His front feet patted the ground again. Suddenly he began slapping the dirt around like mad. Clods and dust flew everywhere. When he realized that he *was* moving down into the earth, he went crazy.

"Slow down a little, Spike. You're going to wear yourself out. Tiger's got to think you've been patrolling. He can't get suspicious yet."

"Oh, yeah. Hey, this is pretty fun. Wonder why I hadn't thought of it sooner? I could have been out of here long ago." Spike shook the dirt from his back.

"I don't know. Probably nobody ever showed you before. I had lots of good digging teachers at home. I'm almost finished with my side. When you get back, I'll go keep Tiger busy. Right now you'd better go check on him again. We're too far along to get caught now." I kept digging.

When Spike returned, my opening was perfect. I had dug under the fence and taken out enough dirt, so all he had to do was break through the surface.

"Tiger is clear on the other side of the yard, chasing a rat in the woodpile," Spike announced. "That should keep him occupied for a while. I'm ready to dig. Are we almost done?"

"Check it out. I have most of the dirt pulled from below you. All you have to do is dig down and break through to the big opening I made. Get after it, Spike!" I stood back a little.

"Here I go!" Spike started clawing into the earth. The dirt flew and hit the ground with a loud *swoosh* after *swoosh*.

I trotted to the far side of the junkyard. Ears perked, I listened for the big dog as I sneaked toward his patrol area. I heard him talking to the rat.

"Come on out, little guy. I know you're in there. I won't hurt you. Come see Tiger." The mean dog licked his lips as he rustled through some trash. I dropped to my stomach and watched as he sniffed and snorted through the pile.

Certain he was still busy, I headed back to Spike.

I was almost to our big trench when I heard Tiger yelp. Running as fast as I could, I got back to Spike. He was almost out! I jumped into the ditch and started digging from my side. We only needed another inch or so.

My sharp ears could hear Tiger coming toward us. Panting and puffing, the beast was moving closer and closer.

"Dig, Spike!" I yelped at him.

"I'm digging. I'm digging!" Dirt flew everywhere as we both clawed frantically.

For an instant I stopped digging and peeked up. The huge, mean dog lumbered toward us. His teeth shined yellow in the moonlight. His powerful jaws opened. His tight eyes aimed right at Spike's rear end.

CHAPTER 4

"Aarraug! I'll get you, you nasty little dog!" Tiger slobbered as he charged toward Spike's rear end.

"Take a deep breath and dive!" I yapped at Spike. "You can make it!"

Twisting and turning, the little dog squeezed himself into the hole. The end of his tail flashed through just as Tiger's strong jaws snapped shut.

The big, vicious dog stuck his nose into the hole. Dropping to his elbows, he snorted at the loose dirt. Wide-eyed, panting, and shaking, Spike raced to stand beside me.

"You made it!" I said, kissing him on the

cheek with my tongue. "We did it. You're safe."

Spike looked back. Tiger sniffed the dirt and frowned. With a wag of his tail, my new friend trotted back to the fence. Right in front of Tiger, he turned around and kicked some clods at him with his hind feet.

"I'll get you for this!" Tiger snarled, burrowing into the dirt with his nose.

"No, you won't. You can't ever get me now. You're stuck in there *forever*, and I am free, free, free." Spike turned to me and wagged his tail. "I'm ready, Freddie, let's move out!"

"You're not going to get away with this," Tiger barked. "Roy will get you. He may even send *me* after you." Tiger charged at the fence. Sharp yellow teeth bit and tore at the wire.

Spike stuck his nose in the air. "Nah. He doesn't need me when he has a fine watchdog like you. Look what a great job you did, letting me escape. Besides, now there will be more food for you."

Tiger threw himself against the fence. Teeth bared, his growl grew more ferocious and angry.

"Come on, Spike. We'd better move on." I nudged at the little dog.

"No, this is too much fun. Tiger has been mean to me ever since I got here. He deserves it." Spike's tail flipped back and forth.

I nudged at Spike's rear again. "You're free. Don't be mean. That's not what you're about. Let's go."

"Yeah, I guess you're right. We've got to move on down the road." Spike prissed as we walked away. Tiger stayed even with us, stalking us from the other side of the fence.

Suddenly Tiger spun and ran back to the hole that we had dug. He started clawing at the dirt.

"Come on, Spike. We've got to run."

We sprinted away from the fence and headed for the trees. We ran and ran until we found a small pond. It was muddy and yucky looking, but it was still cool. We lapped the water. Just as I leaned down for another drink, something hit my rear. The force sent me staggering. I had to leap to keep from landing smack on my nose. Paddling for all I was worth, I turned around and swam back for the bank.

"Figured you needed a little dip." Spike's tail wagged so hard I thought he was going to knock his hind legs out from under him.

"You pushed me."

"Right." He nodded. "Look out. Here I come."

Spike sprang right over me and landed with a big splash in the water. Snapping and chewing at the waves, he swam all around before he came back to the bank where I stood.

"Come on. Let's swim down to the far end before we get out," he suggested. "That way, if Tiger *is* following us, it'll be harder for him to pick up our scent."

We dog-paddled to the far end of the little pond, climbed out, shook, then trotted down a dirt road to our right.

"You think he's going to get out of there?" Spike asked.

"No. He's a lot bigger than you are, and you just barely made it. It would take him forever to get the hole wide and deep enough."

Both of us were sure that Tiger wasn't following. Still . . .

* * *

When we first met, Spike tried to act mean. But his eyes were soft and gentle, and even when he growled I could tell he was a nice dog at heart. Tiger . . . well, he was a different matter. He was mean. Not only was he mean, he *liked* being mean. When I thought of his big, sharp, yellow teeth, and his narrow eyes, and the way his lips curled at the sides when he tore into Spike . . . well, my feet just kind of went faster.

"If he does get out, he may take off for freedom," Spike said, more to himself than to me.

"When was the last time he was out of the yard?" I asked.

"I don't *ever* remember him being out. Once you get in that place, you just don't leave."

I don't know how far or how long we traveled, when Spike stopped.

"Hey, what are those lights?" he asked, pointing his nose toward two bright spots.

"Must be a car. Get over to the side. Looks like it's really moving."

"You think it's Roy and Zack?" Spike pressed against me.

"No, but we'd better get over. That guy is

moving fast." I nudged Spike toward the side of the road.

Dirt and rocks showered us as the car zoomed past and down the road. Taillights glowed red as we watched the back of the car disappear into the dark.

"Let's get off this road," I suggested. "I need a nap. Let's head for that thicket." I looked both ways before we stepped across the road. "We'll slip through those trees. If we find a pond or a creek, we can cut through it. That way our scent will change if anybody does come looking for us."

"I'm with you, pal. We need to watch out in here, though. Sometimes the sound of coyote howls that we hear at night comes from this direction. I don't want to meet any of those guys. I've been talking trash to them for a long time. They may recognize my sound and turn us into mush." Spike moved closer to me as we entered the trees.

We had only gone a little ways when he stopped again. "This is far enough." He dropped his nose closer to the ground and sniffed. "Smells safe. Let's sleep here." Spike walked around in circles, patting the grass down for a bed. Suddenly he stopped. His ears perked straight up and he leaned to one side. "Look, Freddie. Isn't that water over there?"

The tall trees in the forest blocked most of the moonlight. I squinted, trying to see what he was talking about. In the distance there was an open spot with no trees or brush. Moonlight glistened and sparkled off something.

"Yeah, I think I see it." We walked toward it with our ears perked, listening for sounds of other animals that might be close by.

Sure enough, it was a pond. It was long and wide. Moonlight danced and shimmered across the surface. We lapped the cold water for a moment, then leaped in.

"This is great!" Spike bit at the smooth water. Ripples turned into waves as the little dog got more excited. He shook his head back and forth. Sprays of white sloshed into the night air.

"Spike, stop. Listen." Ears perked, I tried to recognize a new sound that moved toward us. I just couldn't quite make out what it was.

"Honk, honk, honk!"

We both paddled for the edge of the pond. Once the soft mud was under my feet, I turned to keep an eye on the water as I backed up and eased closer to the bank. "Spike, listen. There is something in here with us!"

"Yip! Yowie!" Spike yelped as he splashed out of the water and bounded high up onto the bank.

"Honk! Honk! Get away from our pond!"

Wings spread, three huge birds suddenly rose up from the water and loomed over me.

"Chill!" Spike barked from the safety of the bank. "What was all that about? Why did you nip me on the tail? We weren't doing anything."

One of the birds swam closer to me. The other two headed for Spike. I backed up a bit more.

"You're in *our* pond. Get out! Get away from our babies," the big bird hissed. "We have families to protect. Go on!"

I was surprised how quiet and fast the birds swam up on us. It was even more of a shock to see how fast they moved once they were out of the water. The two splashed and sloshed onto the bank after Spike. He yipped again when one nipped his tail with her beak. A long neck stretched out toward me. I spun and took off. The beak kept snapping right at my tail when I sprang from the water and raced to join my friend, high up on the bank.

"What were those things?" Spike panted.

"Geese." I glanced behind us to make sure they weren't still following. Two of the shapes glided across the water, back to where they had been. "My boy and I used to see them when we went for walks in the park. He would give them pieces of bread, and they would follow us all over. When he finished feeding them, they would chase us. They can peck pretty hard. We need to move on even though I don't think they will come after us. They have babies to protect."

The thought of my boy and the fun we used to have made the sadness tug at my heart. Suddenly the goose who had chased me from the pond spread his wings and charged. The sadness was forgotten. I spun and took off with Spike right behind me.

"I was just starting to have fun in there." Spike shook his wet fur.

"Me, too."

My ears perked as we trotted through the tall trees and away from the lake. As we neared a field at the far edge of the forest, I heard a new sound.

"What is that?" Spike asked, tilting his head to one side.

"Cows."

"Cows?"

"Yeah. They are these big animals that eat grass."

"Are they dangerous?"

"No," I answered with a shrug of my ears. "They just stand around and eat and swish flies with their tails. They're big. I guess they could be dangerous if they stepped on you. If we're quiet, maybe we can slip through without bothering them."

We tucked our tails and quietly eased our way out into the opening. The big creatures stood very still, some with their heads up, some with their heads down. They must have been asleep on their feet. We crept along silently. Spike stayed right in my footsteps. At least I thought he did.

By the time I realized he wasn't following me, it was too late.

"Hey, look, Freddie," Spike's bark knifed through the night. "This guy is just about the same size as us. Isn't he cute?"

My eyes flashed wide. "Spike!" I gasped. "Get away from him, now!"

"Moooooo." The sound that came from the little animal was more like a cry than a bellow. It was all it took.

"Mooo rooow!" Suddenly a big cow stood, glaring down at Spike. "Get away from my baby."

Then, before I knew what was happening, there was more mooing and bellowing than I had ever heard in my life. The very ground seemed to shake beneath my feet as the whole herd rushed toward us.

In the blink of an eye we were surrounded. The enormous animals towered above us. Their soft brown eyes were so tight and filled with anger that they seemed to glow red in the moonlight.

We were in big trouble!

CHAPTER 5

Spike and I backed up until our rear ends bumped together. Then we backed up even farther, until we were practically sitting on each other's rumps. All around us cows snorted and bellowed. Pitching their big heads toward the sky, they kept stepping closer and closer. With each step, we pressed harder against each other, until we were almost a ball.

"Hey, Spike, we've got to get out of here," I whispered, shoving him toward the trees. Spike didn't move.

"Sounds great, but how? That one has really sharp things on his head. Looks like the poky sticks they used on me at the junkyard."

I took a deep breath. "Get ready. When I say go, stay low and head for the trees. These guys are big, but they aren't as fast as we are. Just keep running."

"I don't know. They're everywhere!" Spike shivered and pressed even harder against my bottom.

"Just take off, and don't look back. Ready? GO!" I barked.

Spike leaped forward so quick, and I was leaning against him so hard . . . well, I almost fell over backward. I managed to catch myself and spin around to follow as he raced into the circle of cows. I was hot on his heels. I stayed so close that his tail kept flopping me in the nose as we ran.

Dodging and darting, we wove between twenty cow legs. An enormous hoof flashed at the corner of my eye. I ducked and leaned to the left. Just in time! The hard hoof was so close it brushed my whiskers but didn't hit my head.

A huge head ducked at me. I heard the sharp point slice through the air. The horns just missed my back. Slobbers from the mouth landed against my side. The snorting and mooing was so loud, it was like a wall of noise. How we managed to escape and make it to the brush . . . I still don't know.

We ran and ran and ran until we could hardly breathe.

"We can stop now, Spike," I wheezed.

"Nah, let's keep going," he panted. "I don't want to see those guys again. They may get us if we slow down."

"We can go a little farther." I had to pause and suck in another breath. "But they should be settling down for the night. We need to get some rest, too."

We ran a while longer, then slowed to a trot. Finally we walked. We were well clear of the cow pasture when we finally found a safe place to sleep.

The rest of the night was uneventful. When we awoke the next morning, we found about five different trails that branched out from near the spot where we rested. We sniffed at each of them. Some were well traveled, some not. I didn't want to cross paths with anyone unexpectedly, so we trotted down the path that had the least traffic.

"What's for breakfast, Freddie?" Spike asked after a while.

"I haven't seen a thing. No garbage dump or trash can. No place where people throw things away. We may have to chow down on grasshoppers."

"Yummy, my favorite!" Spike's nose curled to a disgusted sneer. "I'm thinking I should have stayed at the junkyard. This isn't working out very well."

He stopped to scratch at one of his fleas. I turned back and stood beside him.

"I thought we'd see a house by now, too. I just can't believe we haven't—"

A sudden noise made me stop right in the middle of what I was saying. My ears stood straight up. Spike's did, too.

"Do you hear that?"

"It's another dog, isn't it?"

"I think so." I nodded. "And if it's a dog, there has to be food for him to eat."

"Let's go find out," Spike said with a wag of his tail.

"We'd better be careful. He may be like Tiger or worse," I cautioned.

"Thanks for reminding me about Tiger." Spike's head drooped and his tail stopped wagging.

The barking sound led us to a little hill. We flattened ourselves on the ground and crawled on our bellies to peek over the top. Below us, in a little valley, we saw a house with a short wooden fence around it. The dog was barking at something in a tree.

"He looks pretty big to me, Freddie. Not as big as you, but he looks old, and mean, and cranky, and . . . and . . ."

The barking stopped and the dog ran to the fence and looked our way.

"Grrrr ooow! Stay away from here." He snarled as he bounced against the fence.

"This isn't the right place for us, Spike. We'd better move on." I slowly backed away from my perch on the hill.

The next house looked friendly, until a thin man came running out of it, yelling at the top of his voice.

"Get out of here, you mongrels!"

Spike and I tucked our tails, but we didn't run away.

"I mean it! Go on, get!" He waved his arms in the air.

"Let's go a little closer, it may be okay." I dropped and wagged my tail. "Maybe if I look sweet and friendly . . ."

"Oh, I see how it is." The man turned and marched back into the house.

"Maybe he's going for some food." Spike's tail wagged.

We sat still for just a few seconds. All at once my eyes flashed wide when I saw the shiny metal stick in his hands.

"No, I don't think so," I yelped. "Run, Spike! Run for your life!"

Kaaa-blam!!!

Tiny lead pellets peppered the grass and weeds, just inches behind our rumps.

"I guess he means business," Spike said when we finally stopped running and cowered near some bushes.

"Yeah, he's serious, but he shot behind where we were. I don't think he really wanted to hurt us."

"Yeah, right." Spike huffed. "Just his way of telling us to go away."

"Right." I shrugged my ears.

Spike licked his front paw. "We have to find something. Maybe a road with more cars? People throw food out all the time. Meat, bread, other stuff."

"Yum, that sounds almost as good as grasshoppers." Just the thought made my tongue rub against the roof of my mouth, like I was trying to get rid of some nasty taste or something.

Spike nudged at my head. "Come on. Let's give it a try."

The road wasn't any good, either. Every piece of paper was just a smell. No bites of food, not even a crumb. So—it was back to the field and—grasshoppers. They were crunchy and full of protein. But the taste wasn't exactly what I'd call yummy.

Exhausted and still hungry, we found some dried grass near a plum patch. We walked around in circles, patting it down to make our bed.

"I'll keep first watch." I arched my neck to check the area.

"Okay. I'm pretty tired." Spike rolled himself into a ball, but managed to still touch me at the same time. His eyes closed and he was sound asleep. I listened to the noises around me. I don't know what happened, but I must have dozed off, too.

"*Woof, woof, grrr, woof, woof.*" Soft barking sounds woke me up.

My eyes popped open and I looked around. Spike was on his back, his feet in the air. He was as relaxed as could be. He was still asleep, but he was barking and growling at something.

"*Woof, woof, grrr, woof, woof,*" he yipped again.

I jumped up and looked down at him. "Wake up, Spike, you're dreaming."

"Huh? What?" The little dog flipped over and struggled to his feet. "What?"

"You're dreaming, dog. Barking and growling at something. It must have been pretty scary." I nuzzled him.

"Can't remember anything." Spike yawned. He blinked a couple of times and shook his head. "It couldn't have been too bad."

"Lie back down. Try to get some sleep," I said.

"That's easy for you to say. I *was* asleep and you woke me up to tell me I was sleeping. That doesn't make any sense. Now you tell me to get some sleep. Besides that, I'm hungry." Spike scratched his head with his front paw.

"Yeah." I sighed. "Me, too. We should be able to find something tomorrow." I snuggled up against Spike.

My ears suddenly stood up on end. "Do you hear that?"

Spike twisted his head, listening to the scratching sounds in the grass. We both stared into the dark. The sound came closer.

"What is it?" Spike whispered. "I can't see anything."

"I don't know, but I think it's coming this way."

As we peered into the night, two creatures rustled out from some tall grass and into a little clearing. Long snouts scraped the ground in front of them.

"I can't see anything." Spike sat up on his haunches and stared at the brush. "What is it?"

My eyes flashed wide.

"What is it?" he repeated.

My eyes just got bigger and bigger, but I couldn't answer.

"Freddie," Spike snapped. "What is it?"

"Don't know. They're not bobcats or coyotes. The things are really weird. They have a long pointy nose on one end, little pig ears, and a hard covering—kind of like . . . like . . . well, I don't know what it's like. It's all over their bodies. Then there's this long pointy tail and . . . I've never see anything like it."

"Scoot over, let me see." Spike shoved me aside with his shoulder.

"Maybe we'd better just get out of here." I scooted farther in the other direction.

Spike's tail started to wag. "No, it's okay. These guys are funny. Just watch. They get scared really easy." Slow and quiet, he moved toward them.

The big animals dug and burrowed into the soft earth, never looking up. I was careful to keep Spike between me and the weird creatures.

Spike crept out of the bushes and crouched down in the path of the animals. The two big things moved slowly toward him. Snouts down along the ground, they sniffed and rooted in the leaves. Spike was perfectly still as they moved nearer. Well, almost. His tail flipped just a bit, and his whole rear end wiggled back and forth. Ears perked, he almost seemed to tremble with excitement. The two animals were so busy concentrating on sniffing the leaves and dirt that they didn't even see him. Their noses almost touched when Spike suddenly jumped up on all fours.

"Grrrrrr. Get! Get out of here!" Spike barked furiously.

Eyes and mouths as wide as could be, the two big creatures stared blankly at Spike. Then—before I could even blink—they jumped straight up, spun around in midair, and bounded back into the brush. I blinked a couple of times. It was hard to believe something that clunky looking—heavy and all covered with a hard shell—could move that fast. Long tails dragged behind their hard backs as they scooted out of sight.

Spike and I laughed as the two animals disappeared.

"What were those things? How did you know they would run away?" I stared into the dark brush.

"Those are armadillos. They're pretty harmless to us. They used to come around the junkyard at night. They dig in the dirt for insects to eat. The best part is that they scare so easily. Did you ever see anything as funny as those guys? I'll bet they are still scooting through the field." Spike was laughing so hard he had trouble standing on all four legs.

"*Grrrrrowl!*"

The sound came from behind us. The hair on the back of my neck stood straight up.

"What are you two bag of bones doing in *our* forest?" Deep voices came from the trees.

Not blinking. Not even breathing. Spike and I spun around and stood plastered together as the voices came closer.

CHAPTER 6

"Let's get 'em, boys!" Sharp white teeth shone in the moonlight as the creatures moved closer.

"We're not doing anything, leave us alone," I pleaded.

"*You* don't have to do anything, we'll do it all." The mangy-looking coyote licked his lips and leered at us.

"Yeah, relax. We know what we're doing." Another one of the beasts ambled closer.

I shook so hard, I thought my tail was going to fall off—then my paws and then my legs. Spike just stood beside me. His tail wagged, slow and easy, like he didn't have a care in the world. I took a deep breath and tried to act brave.

"Listen, guys, we're just passing through. We aren't here to cause you any trouble. We're leaving, okay?" Fluffing up my fur, I tried to look as big as I could.

"We know what you are doing. We've been watching you." The biggest coyote stepped to his right, closer to me.

I stood my ground but I could hear my stomach grumbling. "Then you know that we're not here to cause you any trouble."

"Trouble. You dogs are always trouble. Right now you're trying to get our food." The coyote flipped one ear. His fur was drab and dirty.

Two more coyotes moved in from the trees. None of them looked any better than the first two. Hunger still gnawed at my insides. I felt weak and tired and scared, as I tried to pretend to be strong and brave. There were four of them, small but wily, and they knew their way around the country. There were only two of us, one big, one little. I had been in some dog scuffles in town. Usually, I could talk my way out of them. For some reason, these guys looked and acted a lot different from town dogs.

"Come on, gang, let's get them." They circled closer.

Spike just smiled at them.

I heard a gulping sound when I swallowed. "Hey, guys, let's talk this over. I'm bigger than three of you put together. My pal here—he's a junkyard dog. The toughest kind of dog in the world. You know that. Junkyard dogs are mean and vicious. They just don't get any worse." I looked at Spike. "Look mean," I whispered.

Spike just wagged his tail.

Suddenly the coyotes stopped.

"Junkyard dog?"

I nodded my head so fast and hard that my ears flopped. "Yeah. Junkyard dog."

The big coyote puffed out his chest. "I don't believe it. He doesn't look tough enough to be a junkyard dog. What's your name?"

"Look mean," I urged my friend again.

Spike ignored me. He strolled toward the coyotes, as if they were nothing more than harmless puppies. The four animals sneered at him. Almost to where they stood, Spike sat on his rump and scratched at a flea.

"I don't like to be called 'The Junkyard Dog.'" He gnawed at the flea with his teeth. "It's not a very pretty name. I like my real name better."

The smallest of the four coyotes took a step back.

"What is your name?"

Spike yawned and stretched. I felt my eyes flash wide when he lay down, right in front of them. They could pounce on him. They could be all over him faster than a hummingbird's wings could flap. There was no way I could fight them by myself. What in the world . . .

"You don't happen to know a coyote by the name of Lop, do you?" Spike rubbed his cheek against the ground. "I met him one time. Always wondered what happened to old Lop."

All four of the coyotes took steps backward.

"What's your name?" the big one asked in a muffled growl.

Suddenly Spike was on his feet. He puffed himself up and wagged his tail. He was twice as big as usual.

"You know me already, don't you, fellows."

Spike looked amazing. His eyes narrowed to tiny black dots, and his fur stood up in a ragged ridge down his back.

"You're not . . . not . . . you're not *Tiger*, are you?"

Spike's tail fanned the breeze. "I always wanted to meet up with old Lop again," he said. "I didn't really mean to get his ear." Spike smiled so big his teeth glistened. "I was trying to get his whole head in my mouth. You don't know where I could find him, do you? Are you guys related to him by any chance?"

The coyotes spun around and took off. Only problem, they had eased closer and closer together as they watched Spike. When they tried to run, all they could do was bump into one another. They crashed and thumped and bumped, managing to end up in a tangled pile of paws and tails. Snouts snapping, frightened voices yapping, they rolled and tumbled on the ground.

Then . . . they were gone. The only thing left was a cloud of dust that swirled around us, then drifted off into the night.

Mouth wide, I looked at Spike again. His fur

was down and his eyes were soft again.

"What in the world? How did you do that?" I asked.

"Don't know. I really don't know. Coyotes come around the junkyard all the time. They come to the fence and try to get our food. They can't get in, so Tiger always talks real ugly to them. He got that one called Lop, by the ear, one time. I think that's why they named him Lop—because he only has one ear and he looks kind of lopsided. Anyway, after that they never got near the fence again. Coyotes do a lot of howling. Guess word got around, real quick, about Tiger."

"How did you manage to act so cool and calm? Weren't you scared?"

"Sure I was scared," Spike admitted. "But I couldn't let *them* know that. I had to make them believe I was Tiger and ready to eat them up."

Just watching him and thinking how fast the cowardly coyotes took off, I felt brave as could be. "Hey, I think we could have taken them. You're pretty big and strong and—"

"Forget it!" Spike interrupted, shivering. "We have to get out of here. They might come back." We took off in the opposite direction from the coyotes.

We kept our pace for a mile or so before we stopped for a quick dog nap. It was getting light when we woke up. With both of our tummies growling, we headed back toward the road.

We hadn't been walking very long when we had to make another decision. Our road turned into gravel and dust. We either had to head back toward the town or keep looking in the country.

"There's more people in town, so that means more food. Houses aren't very close around here." I sat and stared at Spike.

"That's all true, but more people might recognize me. Then they'd send for Roy and Zack if we go back toward town. Let's take our chances in the country. I really don't want to go back to the junkyard." Spike jumped up. "Ready, Freddie?"

We were dog trotting when we sighted another farmhouse. We crouched down and watched for a long time. We could see a big fence surrounding the yard behind the house.

Another fence divided that, making a smaller pen. There were two wooden doghouses there, and instead of green grass, the area was mostly dirt.

"Yip, yip!" Friendly sounds came from the smaller pen.

"Look, Freddie. There's a couple of dogs. They look big, but they sound rather nice. Don't you think so?" Spike started to get up.

"Keep your seat, Spike Dog, let's watch a little longer." I didn't want to take any more chances. We needed to save all of our strength just in case we had to walk some more.

Wagging their tails, the dogs watched us. After yipping an invitation to us, they would walk around their pen and sit down. Stomachs growling, we finally decided to check the place out.

As we got closer the two dogs stood up to get a better look at us. Their tails whipped back and forth so fast, they almost knocked each other down.

"Hey, come closer. We can't get out, but we want to meet you." The two dogs sniffed at us through the fence.

They were about the same size. One was a pointer bird dog, the other one . . . I wasn't sure. She was black, but she was getting gray around the face. Her hair was pretty short and her long tail was just a little furry.

"Hey, what took you two so long? We've been waiting for you." The black dog stuck the tip of her nose through one of the chain-link squares.

"Waiting for us? What for?" Puzzled, I stepped even closer to the fence.

"We haven't had a . . ."

Before she could finish, a man strolled around the side of the barn. The instant he saw us, he bent over and picked up a big stick from the ground. Shaking the thing at us, he yelled at the top of his voice:

"Get out of here! Go on. You two have to go. Scat! You can't stay here."

Spike was in front of me as we charged for some nearby trees. Behind us, we heard the girl dog barking.

"Wait. Don't leave," she yapped. "He doesn't really mean it."

"That was close." Spike panted. "That man

didn't look very friendly, but the dog said they were waiting for us. What do you think she meant?"

"I don't know. Just keep going. We can rest behind those rocks." I nudged Spike.

After we caught our breath and settled down for a few minutes, I jumped up and started sniffing. Rocks were piled up on mounds of dirt. It seemed strange to me, and I didn't recognize the smells that came to my nose.

"Get over here, Freddie! There's somebody coming. It doesn't look like the crazy guy with the stick, but we'd better hide anyway." Spike huddled behind a stack of rocks. I snuggled down next to him to watch.

"Pup. Here, pup. Come on, I know you're here somewhere," a soft voice called out.

"Bethany, come back here! They're gone now. We don't *need* another dog! Besides that there were two of them." A deep voice called after her. "I'll have to get a second job just to buy the dog food we'll need. Come back . . . please."

"Oh, Andy, how much could two little dogs eat?"

"Plenty. That one dog is huge. I'll bet he can eat a bag a week. Please come back," the man begged.

The woman just giggled at him.

"He's got to be starving then. Big dog, little dog, hungry dogs. We've got to feed them." She moved closer to our hiding place.

"We already have four dogs." The man sighed. "We're not a dog shelter. They probably have ticks and fleas. Let them go."

The woman's soft hazel eyes seemed to light up when she spotted us. "I can see them. Come here, Andy. Look how cute they are."

"Jake and Ding were cute when you let them stay," the man grumped. He reached out for the woman's arm.

"Jake and Ding are still cute," she snapped, pulling her arm away. "I love them. You know they are wonderful dogs. They make me laugh every day." With a smile, she turned, grabbed the man, and gave him a big hug.

"What about Biff and Barkie? They are *not* cute." The man tried to look angry and disgusted, but all he could do was smile.

"I know they're not the prettiest dogs in the

world. But they are old and I love them, too. Pugs can't help it. Besides, Biff was your mother's favorite." She kissed him on the cheek.

"Oh, my gosh. I'm running a dog circus here, right?" The man patted her on the head.

"I guess. Come on and help me get these pups fed. After they eat, perhaps they'll leave. They may just be hungry." The woman hugged him again.

"I'm pretty sure you said that with Jake and Ding! As a matter of fact, I'm positive. Oh, well . . . I might as well get this over with. I'll get the pans. See if you can get them over here." The man kissed her on the head and shuffled back toward the house.

"Here, puppies. Come on, we'll get some food and water for you. Come on." The woman crouched down, reached out her arms, and wiggled her fingers at us.

I perked both ears.

"What are you thinking, dog?" Spike growled soft in his throat. "You don't know her, or him. How can you trust them?" The fur ruffled on his back.

I felt my tail wag as I watched the woman and her gentle smile. "Sometimes, you just have to take a chance." I sighed. "She looks really nice. He can't be too bad. And besides, what about Jake and Ding over there? They said they were waiting for us." I looked at the two dogs standing by their fence. Their tails wagged and wagged.

"Come on, you two. Let's get some food." The woman moved closer and touched the top of my head. Spike stood tall and let out a timid growl.

"Relax, Spike. I'm starving. She's going to feed us. If we don't want to stay, we'll leave. We're hungry and she's offering food. Think about it." I shoved my nose under her hand.

"Good dog. What a sweetie." She rubbed my ears and face.

"How can you trust *people*? You loved your boy and you got dumped. Now you're going to trust these humans? You don't even know them. I think we'd better go." Spike's fur was still in a ridge across his back.

"Listen, Spike Dog. You know a lot of things, but I am hungry. Get it? Free food. No grasshoppers. No garbage." I woofed at Spike. Wagging my tail, I looked up at the lady. She scratched my ears and stood up.

"Come on, pups. Let's find Andy and get some dog food. It's okay. You're safe here."

The bird dog and the one named Ding put their paws on the fence and wagged their tails as we came closer.

"Welcome," the old black dog greeted. "We're glad you're here. What took you so long?"

"How did you know we were coming?" I asked the yapping dogs.

"We knew you were in the neighborhood." The bird dog barked at us. "Most strays who come around this area usually end up here."

"How did you know we were around?" Spike lifted his ears and tilted his head to one side.

"We heard the coyotes talking about you," the bird dog answered with a wag of his tail. "You must have crossed their path last night and—"

"But why did you think we'd come here?" The ridge on Spike's back smoothed down a bit.

"It just happens. Ding ended up here. I ended

up here. Just something about the place and the people . . . I guess. I'm not sure. Something draws dumped dogs."

Tail drooped and still cautious, Spike trotted slowly behind the woman and me.

"I'm still not sure about this," he complained.

"Here it is, Bethany." The man handed two bowls to the woman. "Your collection of dogs is getting out of hand. But here's food for these two barkers."

"Thank you, dear. Look at them. They are starving. I'll let them eat. If they need to go on their way, they can. If not, we'll try to find a good home for them." Bethany set one bowl down in front of me.

"I'm *so* sure they are going to run off as soon as they eat," the man teased. "Life around here is just too easy. That's why they leave—right? Of all the dogs that we've ever had, you've only found new homes for two. Your mother took one and Mr. McDonald took the other. I know what's going to happen. But I love you anyway." He set the other bowl down near Spike. When he reached to pat him on the head, Spike shied away.

Standing up, the man and woman backed toward the house.

I didn't wait. My stomach growled with anticipation as I slurped and gobbled the delicious food.

CHAPTER 7

"I guess I *was* pretty hungry," Spike mumbled, his mouth full of food.

"I think you got that right. It seems like a long time ago that my boy fed me. This is just as good. No, this is better." I woofed down the last few bites.

Bethany and Andy sat on the porch and watched us as we finished our yummy meal. They didn't say anything when we sprawled out under a big tree for a nap. They just got up quietly and went inside the house.

"What do you think, Freddie? Are we safe here?" Spike stretched his front legs out as far as he could. His rump wiggled back and forth as he flipped his tail.

"The food is excellent," I said, licking my front paws. "The people are nice. The other dogs seem happy and they like it here. We're far enough away from the junkyard that I don't think anyone is going to come looking for you."

"It's almost too perfect. Great food. Friendly people. Pleasant dogs. Too perfect." Spike closed his eyes and drifted off to sleep.

I watched for a while, but my eyelids felt heavy. I needed a little rest. Spike and I had walked a long way. For the first time in three days, our tummies were full. A short nap would be perfect.

"Hey, Pupper."

The voice startled me from my nap. My legs tensed, but before I could jump up and run, the woman's soft face smiled down at me.

"We're going for a walk. I don't suppose you two want to go."

My eyes blinked a couple of times and my tail flipped, just a bit, at the warmth of her voice. She held a very small dog in one arm. The man held another one. Both dogs' tongues hung out. I guess that was because their faces were smushed and flat. There probably wasn't enough room in their mouths to keep their tongues inside. Spike woke up with a growl.

"We're taking a walk. You two can stay here or go with us. Your choice." Bethany reached over to touch Spike.

He jumped to his feet and hopped out of reach.

Bethany shrugged. "We're not going far, but we're letting Jake and Ding out. They'll probably want to check you over. Just wanted to let you know."

Andy turned and walked toward the old black dog and the pointer. "I'll get them." Opening the gate, he headed for the pen where the two dogs were. The bird dog jumped straight up in the air as Andy came closer.

My mouth flopped wide and I blinked. The bird dog jumped again. He didn't even run or so much as bend his legs. He just jumped. All fours left the ground at the same time and he went straight up. The big thing hopped so high, he was almost even with the top of the fence. Again and again and again, he bounded into the air. I felt my eyes roll inside my head. It was weird. How could he do that? No matter how closely I watched, his legs barely bent as he popped up into the air. His big floppy ears floated out like the wings of a bird as he came down, only to hop again.

"Woo woo woof!" The black dog bounced toward the gate. She didn't jump like the bird dog. Her hind legs were stiff and could only move with short, tiny steps.

Andy opened the gate and scooted aside.

"Watch it! Here they come."

The two big dogs ran toward us. The white dog started sniffing at me. His nose whiffed so hard it almost sucked in some of my fur. The old black dog finally hobbled her way up to Spike. He bristled, then relaxed when he knew she was friendly.

"Jake! Ding!" Andy shouted. "Come on, let's go. You know the routine." He set the little dog in his arms onto the ground.

The old black dog turned and headed away from us, trotting at low speed.

"Woof! Be back!" The bird dog raced away so fast he left tiny clouds of dust floating in the air.

Even though he wasn't mad or scared, Spike's fur still stood on a ridge down his back. "What was that about?" he asked, crossing his eyes and shaking his head. "And where are they going?"

"I don't know. Want to go with them and find out?" I stood up and checked the food bowl again.

"Let's just hang out here and see what happens. I'm still pretty tired, aren't you?" Spike asked, finally relaxing the ridge of hair down his back.

Although Bethany and Andy carried them home, the two little dogs looked exhausted. Their legs dangled down and their tongues hung out, even farther than before.

"I'll put Biff and Barkie inside," Andy said, taking the two little dogs into the house.

"Come on Jake, Ding. Time to eat," Bethany called, opening their gate.

The bird dog ran to the water bowl. He put

his front paws in the big black bowl and started digging. It was like he was unearthing a bone or something, but he was jabbing at the water instead of the dirt. He dug so hard and fast, it took only seconds for his chest and belly to get totally soaked with the droplets and spray. I guess Bethany and Ding knew his routine. They both waited outside the gate until he shook and threw water all over the pen and the side of the doghouse. When he was finished, Bethany knelt down beside the black dog and rubbed Ding's ears and face. Then she stroked her back and legs. Ding leaned against the woman as she massaged her old shoulders and neck. After a few minutes she fluffed the dog's head one last time.

"Okay. It's time to eat."

Ding gave a shake and lumbered into the pen. She got a big drink before going to her food bowl.

Spike and I stood outside the backyard, watching. Bethany latched the smaller pen where Ding and Jake lived. Then she strolled to the gate where we stood. "Now, what about you two? Are you ready to join us in the backyard or are you still happy out here?" she asked, rubbing each one of my ears, then fluffing the hair on my back. She reached for Spike, but he backed away from her. Bethany stood up. "Not ready yet? It's okay, take your time."

"Don't you want to go in the yard?" I looked at Spike. The hair was up on his back again.

"How can you trust her?" Spike kicked at the dirt. "You don't know anything about these people. You were dumped not very long ago, and here you are, ready to jump into these people's arms. I don't get it."

"I can't sit around and hide. Bethany seems kind and I like her. I just have to see what happens. Besides, I don't like sleeping out in the wild. We were lucky bluffing the coyotes. They may not bluff the next time. You—Spike Dog—need to relax. This could be the best thing that ever happened to you. If you keep acting mean, you might miss it."

I plopped on the ground. Spike's lip curled and his whiskers raised up on one side of his mouth.

"You're cute and fluffy. Big—but cute. I'm just a junkyard dog. They will keep you and send me on my way. What will I do then?" Spike lay down and dropped his head to rest on his outstretched paws.

"You've had some hard times, Spike. Remember what your life was like before you went to the junkyard. That wasn't so bad, was it?"

"No, it was a very good time."

"Then don't worry," I said, thumping my tail against the ground. "We'll just see what happens. If things don't turn out well, we'll just travel some more. Is that okay with you?"

"I guess." With his chin resting on his paws, Spike's nose was so close to the ground that a puff of grass and dust spun up when he sighed. "Let's catch a nap. We'll wait and see. I guess we *are* due for something good, right, Freddie?"

"Right, Spike."

We spent the rest of the day under the trees in the front yard. That night we could hear coyotes howling in the valley. We slept, curled together in a pile, close to the porch.

The sky was just beginning to brighten when

Bethany let Biff and Barkie out the front door. Spike jumped up and ruffed his back. I stood up to greet them. They were running as fast as their little legs would carry them.

"Grrrrr. Get back. Give us some space," Spike rumbled the warning, deep in his throat.

"Space? *You're* in *our* space." Biff sniffed at my legs. Then he walked right under me. I nudged him with my nose, then I stretched out on the ground.

"Yeah. This is our home. We were here first. We can sniff all we want." Barkie stared straight into my eyes.

"Hey! Leave them alone." Bethany scolded as she trotted into the yard. "They aren't ready for you two, so early in the morning." She gently shoved Biff back with her foot as she lifted Barkie up into her arms.

She carried the chubby little dog to another part of the yard. The instant his feet touched the ground, Barkie began to sniff the grass. Biff ran to him, trying to sniff and find out if he had discovered some new smells on the ground. The little dogs took turns trailing each other.

Bethany knelt down between Spike and me.

"What are you two sweeties doing?"

Spike eased away as Bethany reached to rub his ears.

I liked being rubbed. If Spike didn't, that was his problem. I jumped up and leaned against Bethany. With a little giggle, she started stroking my head. She massaged my neck, then my shoulders. After that she scratched my back and sides.

"Hey, you two!" Suddenly she jumped up and ran to the fence where the little dogs were digging. "Let's go in. I don't have time to fill up holes."

I watched as she carried one of the little dogs and scooted the other one with her foot. The door shut behind them.

"Those little dogs look funny and they act so mean for little squirts." Spike moved closer again.

"Ah, they're okay. They're pretty curious, and I don't think they really want to harm anybody. They have to act tough. They were here first and they *are* inside dogs. Those two don't know anything about what it's like to be out in the real world." I stretched out in the sun.

* * *

The sunlight was warm on my fur. I don't know how long I slept. The sound of Jake's barking woke me up. Spike hopped to his feet and started looking all around.

"It's the bird dog. Something must be bothering him. Let's go see." I shook my woolly coat as I stood up.

The pen that held Jake and Ding was on the back edge of Bethany and Andy's yard. Skirting the outside of the fence, we walked closer. The dog was barking at something in the tree. He wouldn't stop. Ding couldn't care less. She was stretched out in the dirt near a doghouse.

"Hey, what are you barking at?" I asked the big dog.

"Uh? What?" Jake turned to look at us.

"What are you barking at? I don't see anything in that tree." I stared up at the branches.

"Oh, it's just that obnoxious squirrel. He comes in here about twice a day. I would appreciate it if he would get his own tree. As a matter of fact, he has a whole grove over there. Acorns, pecans—any kind of tree he could possibly want. This old tree barely has leaves.

Why he wants to come in here and stare down at us, I'll never know. Besides that, I just need to bark sometimes. He rattles those leaves and I just can't help it." Jake slurped from his water bowl.

"Why don't you get to run in the big backyard?" Spike's nose touched the fence.

"I don't really know." Jake shook his head. His ears flopped.

"You *do* know, Jake." Ding stood up and stretched out her front legs.

"What? Oh, yeah. I guess I do." Jake pushed his nose through the wire, in the chain-link fence, to give us a sniff.

"Okay. I'll ask again," Spike said with a jerk of his tail. "Why don't you get to run around in the whole backyard? It looks really nice on the other side of the fence."

"Sure . . . okay . . . ah . . . well, somebody has a little digging problem." Jake's shoulders slumped as he turned and crawled in one of the doghouses.

"*Who* has a digging problem?" Ding looked in the doghouse at Jake.

"Somebody." Jake pouted.

"Tell them!" Ding growled back at the doghouse.

"Okay. I guess *I* have a little digging problem. I start digging and I just can't stop. I start looking for treasure and I just have to keep digging. I can dig all that I want to in here. I have a great spot over there. When it's hot, I just dig it out a little. When it gets uncomfortable, I just dig a little more." Jake's head drooped on the floor of his doghouse.

"Truthfully, he has a *big* digging problem." Ding sighed. "I don't know where the dirt goes. Andy tries to fill the holes back in, and there's never enough dirt."

I tilted my head to one side. "Why are you in here? Do you have a digging problem, too?"

"I'm here to keep him company. When I was young, I used to patrol the place at night. You know—keep coyotes and raccoons and skunks away. But to tell you the truth, it's pretty comfortable to be all cozy in here when the coyotes are howling."

"How did you get here?" I asked the old dog.

"I was pretty young when I got dumped. Lots of places that I went didn't want me.

This place . . . well, I was lucky enough to get to stay. Bethany and Andy hadn't lived here very long. They already had three dogs then."

"Jake, Biff, and Barkie? Right?"

"No." The old dog shook her head, then walked around in a couple of small circles before she lay down in the dust. "Jake's only been here for a couple of years. Biff and Barkie belonged to Andy's mother. She died last year. They used to come visit with her. Then they had to live here. They try to sound grouchy, but they are really okay."

"They seem to be all right," I said with a shrug of my ears. "They just don't know us very well yet."

Spike moved closer to the fence. "What about you, Jake?"

"It's kind of hard to remember. We were out hunting for birds. I had pointed lots of quail, things were going pretty good. I guess I took a wrong turn, but I kept hunting. When I looked up, Robert was gone. I was exhausted when I got here. Andy fed me and Bethany petted me. They made a nice pen for me. Lots of people came and looked at me, but not Robert. So I got to stay!"

Jake stood up in his doghouse, turned around, and flopped back down in the straw and bedding.

"Where are the three dogs that were here when you came, Ding?" I looked at the old dog.

"You're a smart dog. You know what happens when you get old, right? We don't live forever. Just like all living things, new life comes along, and the old have to make room for them. Bethany and Andy have a special place for us when we die, out there under the trees. Some people just dump dead animals. Bethany and Andy bury their pets, then put up rocks and markers so that they will remember the special times we had together." Ding stretched as she got up.

"That's kind of sad," Spike whimpered.

"No, it's really great. None of us can stay forever. It means that we are important enough that they will remember us for a long time after we are gone. I'm glad that they will make a special place for me when I die. I don't want them to be sad. I'm glad that they will remember the good times that we had together." Ding took a mouthful of food before she settled back down in the dirt.

Spike plopped on his rump and his eyebrows kind of scrunched down.

"You trust these people, don't you?"

Ding's tail gave a little wag. "I trust them a lot."

Spike seemed to bristle. "I lived in a junkyard and the people there weren't much fun. As a matter of fact, they were downright mean. Then we were on the road, and that wasn't any fun, either." He rubbed his tongue against the roof of his mouth. "Grasshoppers are crunchy," he mumbled, more to himself than to them, "but they taste yucky."

"Bethany and Andy are okay. You can trust them. They will take care of you. Andy gets a bit upset with her when she tries to take care of too much stuff. She always tries to find a good home for lost pets. If it isn't the right place, she won't let them go. She has a kind heart. This is a good place."

CHAPTER 8

A few mornings later sunlight was already streaming through the trees, when the front door opened wide. Bethany and Andy brought the little dogs out. Spike lay beside me, rolled in a ball in the grass. I flopped to my stomach and perked my ears.

Bethany led Biff out onto the grass and set Barkie down. "Go on. Do your morning doo, doggers." She smiled.

The little dogs stretched and headed for the fence.

Andy sat down on the front steps. Beside him was a flat tray with rows of little plants in it. He and Bethany had been working in her flower garden. He scooted some of the garden tools aside and frowned. "I think Barkie's arthritis is bothering her. Those old legs aren't working like they should."

Bethany walked over to where we had been sleeping. She always rubbed my ears, then my face. Even when she was in a hurry, she'd scratch my back, then fluff my head. The ridge on Spike's back had finally quit standing up every time Bethany and Andy came near.

The little dogs were busy sniffing the grass. I followed Bethany back to the porch. Against the side of the house was a small table with four flowerpots on top. She turned each pot, just a little, so the flowers could get some sunshine, then she sat down beside Andy. I nudged her hand with my nose.

"Didn't get enough of your morning love time?" Bethany laughed, rubbing my face. Then she reached around my neck and snuggled me close.

Andy leaned toward Spike and clapped his hands. "Come on, Tough Guy. Come get your rubdown. You want to be part of this, don't you?" Spike tilted his head to one side and perked his ears. "Come on. You've put this off long enough."

Spike stood as still as he could, then suddenly he raced to the porch. He almost knocked me down as he plopped his front paws on Andy's lap.

"About time you relaxed a little." Andy rubbed the slick fur on Spike's back. Then he scratched behind his ears.

"I have tried to get that dog to let me touch him ever since they got here," Bethany huffed. "Now, here he is practically sitting on your lap. I can't believe it."

"You're a fine-looking dog, Tough Guy!" Andy stroked Spike's back.

"Grrrr," Biff growled. "Get out of our way, you big mutts. We need our time with them." He stood stiff-legged on the edge of the porch.

"Bethany, will you please put them inside? Tough Guy has finally let me get close to him. It's not the best time for those two to get temperamental." Andy snuggled Spike closer.

"Scoot over, Beautiful. Let me get these two out of here." Bethany gave me a quick hug, then scooped Biff and Barkie up off the porch and took them inside. When Bethany came back, she started rubbing my face again. I laid my head in her lap and relaxed. We stayed that way for a long time. I loved the way she stroked and cuddled. I could have stayed with my head in her lap forever. And I would have . . .

Trouble was, Bethany and Andy had a cat!

We had seen the big fuzz ball staring at us from the window a few times. He seemed like a calm cat. He'd just glare at us or the birds who fluttered around the feeder that Bethany kept filled with seeds. Spike watched him, but never acted like he wanted to chase him or anything else for that matter. But this was a little bit different.

Screech, scratch. My ears perked at the sound when something clawed at the screen.

"Are you going to let that cat out?" Andy whispered to Bethany.

Spike didn't move.

Bethany shrugged. "I don't know. These two are being so calm, I hate to spoil the mood. That cat comes out—hard telling what will happen."

"Ah, let him out," Andy urged, pulling Spike

a little closer. "He's a real rugged cat. He won't take anything off these two."

Slow and quiet, Bethany got up and walked to the front door.

"Okay, Deeker, come on out," she said, opening the door just a bit. With her foot, she reached down and scooted a brick into the opening so it wouldn't slam shut.

Tail swishing, the big black cat sauntered onto the porch.

"Calm down, Tough Guy," Andy soothed as he held on to Spike's shoulders. "It's okay."

The hair on my friend's back rose slowly, but he didn't growl or anything.

The black cat looked at Spike. His yellow eyes popped big.

"Phhhhissss!" The black cat arched his back. His tail puffed—tripling in size. Eyes wide, he pressed himself against the wall, almost flattening into the bricks.

"What's the matter with Deeker?" Andy asked, stretching his neck so he could look around at the big cat.

"I have no idea," Bethany answered. "He's been watching them from the window. I mean . . . it's not like he didn't know they were here. Maybe he's uncomfortable, since he usually goes out the back door." Her grip relaxed on me when she could tell I wasn't going anywhere.

Suddenly Spike leaped away from Andy.

My heart sank.

This was the "House Cat." If Spike ate him, Andy and Bethany wouldn't like us anymore.

Spike took off.

The cat took off.

I cringed. *Oh, no!*

Then . . .

Mouth gaping wide, I blinked. Then I blinked again.

Spike wasn't going to eat the cat. Spike wasn't even running toward the cat. He took off for the front yard. Only thing, when he leaped from Andy's grasp, he ran smack-dab into the little black tray of plants that sat beside them. Flowers flew all over the place, and the garden tools clattered across the porch. In the blink of an eye, he was gone.

The cat went the same direction. Instead of jumping off the porch like Spike did, he leaped up onto the little table for safety. The table

rocked. The cat rocked. His tail spun in circles a couple of times as the table tilted, then tipped.

There was a loud clatter when the pots crashed to the ground. It made me blink. When I opened my eyes again—the crazy cat was gone!

Andy's mouth fell open as wide as mine was. "What in the world was that all about?"

Bethany blinked a couple of times. Her mouth was open, too. "He must be afraid of Deeker. And Deeker . . . well, the dog must have scared him . . . and . . . and . . . well, they both took off like crazy."

Stepping over the shattered clay pots, she walked to the corner and started calling for Spike. "Come on, Tough Guy. We won't let that cat get you. Come on."

Andy climbed around the porch on all fours and started scooping some of the dirt back into the little black tray. "I thought things were going to be better. That dog finally lets us touch him, and then he goes totally berserk over a cat. Wacky dog." He paused a second, frowned, then smiled. "Maybe *that* should be his name. Wacky Dog." Andy shook his head. When he looked at the place where Spike disappeared around the house, his eyes kind of rolled. "Running from a little old cat . . ." his voice trailed off as he picked up a broom and started sweeping the porch.

"It'll be better when they meet in the backyard," Bethany said, strolling back from the edge of the porch.

I breathed a sigh of relief, now that all the excitement was over. That Spike's one daffy dog, I thought.

"The backyard is Deeker's space," Bethany went on. "He'll take to these guys. I know he will."

She knelt down to help Andy. They swept the dirt and broken pots into a pile. Then they gathered the little flowers and put them back in the dirt they saved in the black tray. When they were finished, they went inside. Andy closed the door behind them.

I didn't like being all alone, so I trotted to the side of the house to see what had happened to my friend. When I got there, I looked all around, but Spike was no place in sight. I finally spotted him, hiding behind a big oak tree, way out beyond the fence.

"What was that about?" I barked. "Everything was calm and you go nuts. What happened?"

Eyes wide, Spike peeked around the tree trunk.

"Is it gone?"

"Is what gone?"

"That big black thing. It had a huge tail and sharp claws. Didn't you see it? It hissed at us. What was it?" Spike was still shaking when he leaned out a bit farther. "I've never seen anything like that. It was scary!"

Once more he ducked back to hide. I blinked. Then I shook my head so hard, the loose skin on my neck flopped.

"You mean you were afraid of that little cat?"

"Cat? Is that what that thing was? It was going to get us." Spike eased from behind the tree once more.

"Get real!" I trotted toward him, trying really hard to keep from laughing my tail off. "It was just a little bitty old house cat. What's to be afraid of?"

Spike wouldn't leave the safety of his tree. I marched right up and looked him square in the eye. "You scared off those coyotes, remember? Coyotes are dangerous. They were going to eat us, but you just strutted up and chased them away. That was a house cat. Dogs chase cats. Cats run from us, *we don't run* from them."

"Are you sure?"

"Trust me on this one, Spike. Don't chase him, because Bethany and Andy like him. But you don't need to be afraid of a cat. Okay?"

"Okay," he answered—only he didn't sound too sure.

I couldn't believe this crazy mutt. I clamped my lips and nose shut so I wouldn't burst out laughing. Once back in the front yard, I finally found the cat. When everything started falling and crashing, I guess he darted back inside the house. We spotted him watching out the window. Wide-eyed and still all fuzzed up, he ducked down when he saw us looking at him.

We didn't see the cat again until we moved to the backyard. A truck full of men drove up the driveway one morning. Spike went crazy. He snarled and growled and barked. He even bit at the wire fence. Andy came out with a blue leash.

"Okay, you two. We can't have this. These guys are going to be here a few days. We can't have any teeth marks in them." I leaned against his leg and wagged my tail.

Andy ignored me and slipped the blue leash around Spike's neck. "Come on, Tough Guy. Let's go inside the small pen at the back of the yard."

I followed them to the back gate. Andy let Jake and Ding into the big backyard and shoved Spike into their pen. I followed my friend inside and Andy closed the gate behind us. For a minute Spike acted almost sheepish. Head bowed and tail tucked, he wandered around and sniffed our new pen. Then he settled down and relaxed a bit.

That was until one of the men came into the backyard and shook hands with Andy.

Spike leaped up and charged the fence. He hit it so hard, I thought he was going to knock a hole in the chain-link. He growled and snarled and threw himself again and again into the wire.

This was weird. Faced with the coyotes, Spike was cool and calm as could be. When the cat came outside, Spike ran to hide. Now . . .

"Spike!" I barked. "What is wrong with you? Why are you acting so crazy?"

"That man is in Andy's yard. He's touching him."

"So?"

"I like Andy. He's nice to me. He pets me and says nice things to me. I don't want that stranger around him. If he hurts my Andy . . . I'm . . . I'm going to . . ."

Again he flung himself against the fence. He snarled and barked and . . . and . . .

This was scary!

CHAPTER 9

Spike didn't calm down until the men finally got into their pickup and drove away. Only then did the hair slowly flatten out on his back. Jake and Ding just sat by our fence and stared at us.

"Hey, dog. You're going to have serious problems if you keep that up. Guarding the yard is one thing, but you're overdoing it, don't you think?" Ding scratched her ear with her hind foot.

"I have to protect Andy. Those people were in his yard. I have to take care of him." The hair on Spike's back came up just a little.

"That guy wasn't going to hurt him. You got

to think about these things. You're going to get in deep trouble, dog!"

The back door opened and Jake and Ding ran to greet Bethany.

"Hey, doggers!" She dropped down to stroke their faces. After a good rub, she walked over to our pen. "What are you two doing?"

Spike jumped around the pen as she opened the gate and walked in. Quickly she petted him, then she caressed my face and scratched my back and neck before she turned back to Spike.

"Hey, Tough Guy. What are we going to do about you? You got a little carried away when those men came to fix the fence. They're working down in the pasture, but they may need to come to the house occasionally. You can't go bonkers every time they show up." Bethany scratched under Spike's chin and brushed at his tail before she stood up. "Be good doggers."

Jake and Ding walked up to the fence as Bethany started out the gate.

"You're being sweet dogs today," she told them. "Not one single hole in the yard."

Bethany rubbed Ding's ears and patted Jake on the head before she walked back to the house. Spike and I stood in the small pen and watched her. Ding strutted up to us and kicked some grass with his hind feet.

"See. Told you so. If you don't behave, you'll never get out of that cage. They may even get rid of you."

"She's right," Jake said. "This is a great place to live. You got to get with the program, Spike, or you'll be out of here." Jake turned back toward the house. Walking in circles, he finally curled up in the grass.

"Sounds like good advice to me." I shook my fur before I settled down in the dust.

"I really don't know what happens." Spike's ears drooped. "I just get real nervous when a stranger shows up."

Comforting him, I kissed him on the cheek with my long tongue. "We haven't even been here long enough to know who the strangers are."

"Yeah, I guess. But sometimes you just can't be too careful." Spike dropped his rear to the ground, closed his eyes, and sniffed the breeze. I settled down for a little dog nap.

* * *

I hadn't been asleep very long when I heard the creak of the back door. Spike and I both stood up and leaned into the fence. The cat sauntered into the backyard, his tail flipping as he walked. I shot a worried glance at Spike.

Spike moved away from the fence. The fur on his back came up slowly as the cat stepped into the yard and moved closer to our pen. Jake and Ding sniffed the cat, then curled up in the sunshine. Then the cat called Deeker headed toward our small enclosure. I perked my ears as he approached. I heard a faint growl as Spike moved behind me.

"Hey, dog! What's the matter with your friend? I'm not here to cause any trouble. I think we must have gotten off on the wrong paw."

"I'm not sure what happened the other day." Spike stood right behind me, shaking just a little.

"What's going on, dog? I'm not here to hurt you. I want to be friends. This is a super place to live. You don't need to be scared of me. I won't bother you *if* you won't bother me.

Okay?" The cat rubbed against the wire cage.

"Hey, I . . . I don't have a problem with that." Spike's voice shook just a little.

"Good deal. I stay in the house most of the time, so you won't even have to see me. When I come out, I stay pretty close to the backyard. Coyotes, you know. I can usually avoid them, but I don't want to be surprised by one." Deeker stretched out his front paws, then dropped down to the ground. He started washing his legs with his pink tongue.

"I'm . . . I'm really not afraid of you. You just sort of . . . ah . . . startled me. I never met a cat before." Sniffing, Spike moved closer to the fence.

"Most of us are okay. It never hurts to be careful. There are some pretty big cats out there. Usually house cats like me just need a little bit of outdoor time." The cat jumped up when the back door opened.

"Deeker? Deeker? Where are you, cat? Come on back in here," Andy's voice called.

"Got to go. I don't always mind when I get called. You know—I have to remind them who's really boss around here, sometimes—

but I haven't eaten yet. Can't miss a meal! See you later." The cat bounded off toward the house.

Spike and I had lots of good days when Andy started letting us out for morning runs. First thing in the day, he would let Jake, Ding, Spike, and me loose for a short sprint. Ding didn't sprint. She kind of hobbled to the end of the driveway, stretched, and waddled back to the yard. Jake usually ran big circles around her, then made a couple of loops around the front yard. Spike and I explored the trees and brush near the house. We stayed close enough to hear Andy when he called us back into the yard.

This morning we hadn't been out very long when a big delivery truck roared up the driveway. Spike's fur ruffled to a sharp ridge on his back. Andy started calling us to come back in. A low growl came from my friend's throat as Andy put a rope around his neck.

"Calm down, Spike. You'll get us put back in the little pen," I warned him.

"Come on, Tough Guy. He isn't going to

hurt you." Andy pulled Spike back into the yard. Jake and I followed them. Ding sat in the grass near the fence and barked at the big truck.

It was more than Spike could take. He barked and growled at the man who stepped out.

"He's a rowdy one." The man strolled up to Andy.

"He really is a pretty sweet dog. You're right though, I don't trust him with people around." Andy took a package from the man.

Spike kept barking, but he didn't bite at the fence like he did the last time.

"Calm down, Spike." My eyes narrowed when I stared at him. "Andy has control of this."

As the big truck drove away, Andy put the box down and came over to us.

"Look, Tough Guy. I know you are trying to take care of things, but sometimes you get a little carried away. I'll let you know if we need any help, okay?" Andy ruffled Spike's fur and petted my head before he walked off.

After that Spike barked and barked to let

Andy know when someone was coming. As soon as Andy came out of the house, Spike stood at attention, but he didn't bark or threaten anyone.

The next time the deliveryman came, Spike even walked up to the fence and licked the guy's hand.

Things were pretty good after that. We had time out of the yard in the morning. We had romp time with Jake in the backyard. Spike would chase him around and I would hide and jump out at him. Then Spike would chase me and Jake would hide and jump out. Mostly, Ding would sit in the sun and watch. One evening Andy and Bethany even had people come over for dinner. They cooked out and we all got along. Spike didn't bark once while they were in the backyard. He even started acting like he didn't know they were there.

It was pretty calm for several days. That was until the black truck drove up.

At first I couldn't figure it out. Spike stood staring at the road as the vehicle rumbled and puttered toward the house. Suddenly that ridge of fur stood straight up on his back and neck. His ears flattened and he started barking. Well . . . it was more like roaring. It was the most ferocious sound I had *ever* heard.

Spike snapped and snarled at the fence as two men stepped away from the truck.

"There's that rotten mutt. I knew we would find him, sooner or later." My tail drooped when I recognized that voice.

Roy and Zack stomped up to the fence. Spike bared his teeth and snarled.

"Well, if it isn't my little junkyard friend. Where have you been, you mangy mongrel? Did you think you could get away from me?" Roy kicked at the fence.

"Hey, Spike. Calm down," I warned. "He wants you to be mean. Cool it or he'll try to take you back to the junkyard. You don't want that, do you?"

"Hey, Zack. This guy is getting better. I did a good job of training him, don't you think?"

"Yeah, but we'd better get out of here." Zack turned away from the fence.

"We'll be back, Mutt! The sheriff can take care of this. I'll bet these people stole our watchdog." Roy's chuckle was sinister and

mean as he climbed into the truck.

Tires squealing, they backed the truck out of the driveway. Dirt flew when they peeled away.

Spike kept barking at the truck. From his tone, I could tell he would tear the tires off the thing if he ever got the chance.

"Hey, what's going on out here?" Andy stepped out the back door. A towel was wrapped around his waist.

Spike ran over to him and licked his hand. He started jumping up and down. His dirty feet left brown paw prints on Andy's towel.

"What's this about? What's all the racket?" Andy lifted Spike's paws off him and then crouched down to Spike's level. "What's the matter with my little Tough Guy?"

"I've got to get out of here. Roy's going to get me," Spike whined.

"You're okay. Was there something that scared you? I heard you barking, but I was in the shower and couldn't get out here." Andy stood up and walked to the fence.

"It's Roy. He's coming after me." Spike started growling at the fence.

"I don't see anything. Must have been a coyote or something." Andy looked at the little pen in the back. Ding and Jake were huddled against the fence.

"What's the matter with you two?" Andy called.

Tails tucked they ran to him.

"What's going on out here, anyway? I'll get some clothes on and check around the fence." Andy petted me on the back, then rubbed Jake and Ding's ears before he disappeared into the house.

"I have to find a way to escape. Roy will be back. He'll really be mean when he gets me to the junkyard. You've got to help me. He may even take you." Spike shook all over.

"Easy, Spike. Easy. Andy will take care of everything. You've got to trust him." I sat on my haunches staring at my friend. I had never seen him so scared or worried.

"It's pretty hard to trust anyone. People are so difficult. Maybe Andy called Roy. They already have plenty of dogs. I'm just another mouth to feed." Spike's tail tucked under his tummy as he stood, staring at the gate.

"Where did you come up with that one?

Andy and Bethany have *never* been mean to us. What are you talking about?" I looked at Spike's face. It was tight and mean looking.

"People." Spike snorted. (Only his snort sounded more like a whimper.) "You just can't trust anybody."

"Maybe you'd better try. These people are good to us." I licked Spike's face.

"I don't know, Freddie. If I have to go back to the junkyard . . . if they take me . . . It's awful there." Spike finally stretched out. His head still quivered as he pointed to the road.

I guess what happened next was my fault.

We were talking so intensely that we didn't hear Andy when he came back outside. Fact was, I only noticed him from the corner of one eye, when he leaned down to pet Spike. I guess Roy was the only thing on Spike's mind—that and his fear—no, terror—at the thought of having to go back to the junkyard.

Andy took one more step. His weight was on his heel. But when he leaned forward to pet Spike . . . well . . . the front of his foot was right over Spike's tail. I didn't even have time to bark a warning.

Spike's eyes flashed wide as he yelped in pain, sprang to his feet, and whirled around.

My heart sank clear down into my belly when I saw his sharp fangs flash.

Andy yelled.

It was too late!

"Let go of him, Spike," I yelped.

Instantly Spike's jaws sprang open. "Oh, no! I've done it now!"

Tail tucked so far under him that it looked like part of his stomach, Spike scooted to the fence. He looked like he'd been beaten with a club or something, the way he cowered against the chain link with his head bowed so low it almost touched the ground.

"What in the world is wrong with you, dog?" Andy hopped around, rubbing at his leg. "I was just going to pet you. Are you hurt?"

CHAPTER 10

Spike ran to the little pen at the end of the yard. He scooted into the doghouse and shoved himself all the way to the back.

"What's wrong with that dog?" I followed Andy as he walked to where Spike was hiding. He leaned over and rubbed his leg before he looked in. "Hey, buddy. What's going on with you?"

Andy and I peered into the dark opening.

"I messed up—big time." Spike whimpered. "I'm so ashamed. I love Andy. I didn't mean to bite him. I'd never . . ." He broke off, sniffling.

"Hey, Tough Guy. I didn't mean to step on your tail. Are you okay? Come on out and let me look at it." Andy squatted in front of the doghouse. "Silly dog. Come out and let me look you over. Are you really hurt?"

Shouldering my way past Andy, I stuck my head inside. "Spike, you better let him look at you. Are you hurt really bad?"

"Get back. Leave me alone, Freddie. I'm bad news. I bit Andy. He'll get rid of me for sure. And if you're around, he'll dump you, too!" Spike flattened himself against the back of the doghouse.

Spike's words sent a chill racing up my back. *"He'll dump you, too!"*

The words seemed to echo inside of my head. Slowly, one step at a time, I backed away from my friend.

I had been dumped once. I had no idea why— no clue as to what I did to be driven in the car . . . away from my boy . . . and left alone in the rain. I liked people. I needed them. Andy and Bethany were good to me. They petted me and loved me. I couldn't bear the thought of losing that.

Tail tucked between my legs, I slinked to the far side of the yard.

Andy reached in to get Spike. "Come on,

Tough Guy. Let's see if you're hurt."

Spike stuck all four legs out and stiffened his whole body to keep Andy from pulling him out of the small enclosure.

"Come on, dog. I'm going to win this one. You might as well make it easy. I know where the leash is and you are coming out of there." Andy grabbed the back of Spike's neck.

Very slowly, Spike relaxed as Andy dragged him from his house. He looked him over—especially his tail—petted him a bit, then let him go. As soon as he did, Spike shot back into the shadows of the doghouse.

"I didn't mean to step on your tail," Andy said again. "It couldn't have hurt that bad. Something else must be going on. Did something scare you before I came out here? I'll go have a look around." Andy walked out of the gate.

As soon as he was gone, Jake and Ding trotted to the doghouse.

"What's going on?" Ding asked, leaning in to smell Spike.

"It was Roy. He's from the junkyard, and he'll be coming back for me. Andy doesn't understand. He doesn't know Roy."

Even from my hiding place at the far side of the yard, I could understand them.

"Andy will do everything he can to take care of you," Jake assured him. "If Roy comes back, Andy will figure out what's going on. You're safe. He will protect you. He protects all of us."

"But . . . but I bit Andy." Spike sniffed.

Ding shrugged her ears. "It was an accident. You didn't mean to. Andy knows that. He and Bethany are good people."

"You guys are safe," Andy promised when he came through the gate. "Didn't see a thing. Not even a track. You're okay. I've got to get out of here. Bethany will be back before lunch. I'll leave her a note so that she will know that you are jittery about something. Okay, guys?"

The rest of the day I kept an eye on Spike, but I didn't get near him. It wasn't until Bethany got back that he started acting normal again. By evening he was hopping around like nothing had happened. I still kept my distance. I never thought I could love someone as much as I did my boy. But Andy and Bethany were special. For people—they were wonderful. If they sent Spike away for biting Andy . . . If they dumped me, too . . . Just the thought of losing them . . . the thought of being dumped . . . again . . .

The next morning I woke with a start. I heaved a sigh of relief when I realized I was still in the yard. After I stretched, did my morning business, and kicked the grass, I glanced at the doghouse. Spike wasn't in his usual spot. He must have taken off in the night. I yelped for Jake and Ding. Ding slowly pulled herself out of one of the doghouses.

"What's wrong?" Jake came running from the corner of the yard.

"Where's Spike? Did he get out?" I growled. "Did he run away?"

"No, he's in the doghouse out in that pen. He crawled in there in the middle of the night." Jake turned and sniffed the breeze.

Ding waddled up to us. "What's with you two, anyhow?"

"What do you mean?" I cocked an ear.

"You two stick to each other like pancakes

and syrup stick to the roof of my mouth."

My other ear raised. "Pancakes and syrup? What's that?"

Jake wagged his tail. "You'll see. Every time Bethany fixes pancakes, she always makes extra for us. They're really sweet and good and—"

"Knock it off with the pancakes," Ding growled. "I'm talking to Freddie." She glared at me. "You and Spike are good friends. But for a whole day and night, you haven't even been near each other. What's going on between you and Spike?"

I couldn't look at her. I turned to sniff at the fence.

"Nothing's going on. What do you mean?"

"Something's wrong." Ding followed me and nudged me with her snout. "Did you two have a fight or something?"

I curled my tail out of the way and plopped down on my rump. For a long time I couldn't look at her. Finally I took a deep breath.

"He bit Andy. He didn't mean to. But he did. And . . . and if Andy sends him away, he'll send me away, too. I've been dumped before. My boy loved me. I had a nice, safe yard to live in.

Then . . . DUMPED! Nobody loved me. It hurt so bad and . . . if it happens again . . ."

All the fear and hurt and sadness just poured out of me. My story tumbled and rushed like water dashing down a stream, and I couldn't stop it until I had told Ding everything.

She sat next to me all the time I talked. She even leaned her head against my shoulder. When I finished, she kissed me gently on the cheek with her long tongue.

"Except for Biff and Barkie, we're all strays," she said. "Jake and me, the dogs who came before us, the dogs who will come after you—all dumped. That's how we came to live with Andy and Bethany. None of us can forget how it feels, not to be needed or loved, but—"

"Yeah, me, too," Jake interrupted.

Ding shot him a stern look.

"But," she repeated, turning to me. "But you and Spike are friends."

That was all she said. The look in her eye left a chill inside me. It almost made me feel as cold and lonely and empty as I did when I found myself deserted at that park. I didn't like it. For that matter . . . I didn't like me too much, either.

* * *

About thirty minutes later Andy came out of the house. He marched straight to the dog-house and peeked in at Spike.

"Hey, dog. Rise and shine."

Spike jumped up and leaped through the doorway. He nearly knocked Andy over, licking and jumping up on him.

"Calm down, Tough Guy. You need to get some of that extra energy run off. Let's go for a jog." Andy opened the back gate and let us all out for our morning romp.

We had fun checking out all the smells that might have been left by critters which had come in the night. We also chased mice that rustled in the grass. Spike, Jake, and I followed trails in the pasture. Ding waddled along behind, stopping now and then to sniff at some really good odors. When we got back to the house, Andy had just closed us in the backyard when a car drove up the driveway.

Spike ran for the doghouse as Jake, Ding, and I started barking at the sound that was coming closer.

Andy stood at the gate. When the car

stopped in the driveway, he walked out and closed the gate behind him. A man in a uniform stepped out.

"Yes, sir. What can I do for you?" Andy stood at the man's car door.

"I'm Nathan Jones with the Sheriff's Department. We had a complaint come in that you had a stolen dog. It's a trained guard dog." The man looked toward us.

"I don't think we have anyone's trained dog. These dogs are all strays that someone has dumped. You're welcome to look at them." Andy stepped back so that the sheriff man could see us.

I barked a bit more, but Ding howled like she was hearing coyotes or something. Jake's tail wagged. Spike was gone!

"People from town are always letting their dogs loose out here. My wife's real bad about adopting strays. But I don't think anyone would want these guys for a guard dog." Andy reached through the links of the fence to touch my face.

"Are these all you have?"

"No, we have Tough Guy somewhere. He's really just a sweet little dog, though." Holding his hands above his eyes to shield them from the noon sun, Andy scanned the yard. "Tough Guy. Come here, pup."

We all looked around for Spike. He was crouched in the back of the doghouse.

"Let me get him. He couldn't possibly be the one you're looking for." Andy went in the house and came back with a blue leash. He walked to the doghouse, bent over, and looped the rope around Spike's neck. Reluctantly the dog came out.

When they came through the gate, Andy dropped down and started petting him. The sheriff reached over and rubbed Spike's head.

"I don't think any of these could be the one they are looking for. You haven't had any others around here lately have you?" The sheriff man rubbed Spike's face, one last time, and got up.

"We haven't seen one lately. These last two have only been here a few weeks. Dogs get dumped out here all the time. I don't understand what people are thinking. Dogs that count on people for their food can't take care of themselves out in the country. The pound at least tries to find homes for them." Andy took the leash off Spike before he let him back in the yard.

"I'll have to check back with the office. I'm pretty sure this is the address they gave me, but it can't be any of these dogs. They're too sweet and gentle. I appreciate your time. Sorry to have bothered you."

"No problem. Hope you find your stolen dog." Andy closed the gate. We all got a good petting before he went back in the house. That was a close call, I thought with a sigh of relief. Maybe it's over. Maybe we're finally safe.

Jake, Ding, Spike, and I were having a little romp when the black truck drove up the driveway. The sheriff man's car was behind it. Jake and Ding ran to bark at the fence. Trembling, Spike shot into the doghouse in the far pen.

I . . . well, all I could do was stand in the middle of the yard. They had come to take Spike back to the junkyard. If I was with him, they'd take me, too.

Then . . . a chill ran up my spine when I remembered the look in Ding's eyes and her words.

"Spike is your friend."

CHAPTER 11

Racing at full speed, I dived through the door of the doghouse. The wooden floor was slicker than I thought. I tried to stop, but I ended up slamming into Spike, who was huddled against the far wall.

There was a little *whoompf* sound. I guess I sort of knocked the air out of him. I struggled to get off, and he struggled to get up.

"Beat it," he whimpered. "Save yourself. They'll take you, too. Run!"

"Shut up and listen to me," I snarled. "Do exactly what I tell you. No matter what happens, don't bark or growl. Just look as sweet as you can."

When Andy came outside, Jake and Ding stopped barking. "What's going on out here?" He blinked when he saw the sheriff's car.

"We want our dog back," Roy called from outside the gate. "And we want to be paid for the time you've had him. We could have been robbed while Spike was gone. You owe us money." Roy gawked around, outside the wire, looking for Spike.

"What are you talking about? I don't have your dog." Andy closed the gate behind him and walked to the sheriff man.

"I'm sorry, sir. Mr. Ferguson here says that you do have his dog."

"Which one of them do you think it is?" Andy rested his elbows on the fence and nodded toward the yard. I stood in the doorway of the doghouse, between Roy and the shadows where my friend hid.

"I've seen that one before." Roy pointed at me. "But that's not Spike. My dog's mean. He's a trained guard dog. We've missed that dog's services while you had him. We want him back, and we want to be paid for the time he's been gone. Where are you hiding him?"

"Tough Guy is probably in the doghouse, over there. But I don't think he's the one you're looking for. He's a sweet dog. He's even afraid of our cat."

"Well, let me look at him." Roy's voice was gruff and nasty. "Spike ain't sweet. He's tough. If he ain't still that way, you must have done something to him. We had that dog trained."

"Just a minute, sir," the sheriff man interrupted. "It's not any of these? Is that correct?"

"Nah," Roy said, turning back to the sheriff man.

"Are you positive?"

Roy's lip curled up on one side. "I told you, he ain't out here. This guy must have our dog hidden somewhere. I saw him here the other day."

"When were you here before?" Andy asked the man.

"We were out looking for Spike day before yesterday. The sheriff told us we had to wait until a deputy could come, 'fore we could get him. Now give me my dog." The man started to pull the latch up on the gate.

"Would you please let him see that other

dog," the sheriff man said, stopping Roy from opening the latch. Roy's lip curled again when he looked down. He yanked his hand from the sheriff man's grasp.

"I'll get him." Andy started for the doghouse where Spike was huddled behind me. When he got to our pen, he started to kneel down and reach past me.

I took a deep breath, made the hair bristle to a sharp ridge down my back, and . . .

Let out the loudest, deepest roar I'd ever barked in my whole entire life.

Andy's eyes flashed wide. He yanked his hand back.

"What's gotten into you?" he asked me.

Just the sound of his voice made my tail want to wag. I wouldn't let it. Instead, I squinted my eyes, gritted my teeth, and roared again.

Andy took a step back. Spike growled.

"Don't you hurt Andy. I love him. I never meant to bite him. When I did, I made a promise to myself that I'd never bite anyone or anything, ever again. But so help me . . . if you hurt Andy . . ."

"I'm not going to hurt Andy," I whispered over my shoulder. "Just do what I told you. Don't bark. Don't growl. Don't even show your teeth."

"Not even at Roy?"

"Especially not at Roy!"

Andy shook his head and moved toward our doghouse again. I snarled and barked and snapped. Head tilted far to one side, he looked at me a moment.

"What is wrong with you? You've never acted like this." Andy stomped his foot, snapped his fingers, and pointed to the ground beside him. "You get out here! RIGHT NOW!"

Tail tucked, I slipped through the doorway and went to stand where he pointed. I leaned against his leg and rubbed his knee with my cheek.

"That's the weirdest thing . . ." I heard him say, more to himself than to me.

Spike whimpered softly as Andy reached in the doghouse. "Come on, Tough Guy. You can't be the one these guys are looking for."

Slowly Andy pulled him out. Tail tucked and ears drooped, Spike's brown eyes were wide open.

"Is *this* the mean, vicious guard dog that you've been looking for?" I heard the sheriff ask.

"They must have done something to him. They've probably been hitting him or something. They are going to owe us big time." Roy kicked at the fence when Andy dragged Spike closer.

"Sheriff Jones, I don't think this could be his dog. He's shaking like a leaf. If this man actually had him, he must have been treating him pretty rough." Andy rubbed Spike's ears. Spike's tail wagged just a little.

"Just give me my dog!" Roy's ugly face looked really mean when he started to open the gate once more.

"Just a minute, Mr. Ferguson. I think there's something really wrong here. When I came out this morning, that dog was happy and jumping around. The big fluffy one"—he nodded toward me—"well, he was sweet as could be. Now that you're here, he's like a different dog. The one you claim is your guard dog acts like he's scared of *you*." The sheriff man walked into the yard and squatted down to pet Spike.

Jake, Ding, and I all pushed in close to them. I held my breath, hoping Spike wouldn't growl or bite at the sheriff man. He didn't.

"That's a good dog. You aren't any kind of guard dog, are you, pup?" The sheriff man looked Spike over, then let go of him and petted each of us. As soon as he was free, Spike ran to the safety of the doghouse.

"That's my dog and I'm going to have him. There's laws, you know." Roy puffed out his chest.

"Well, sir, if this is your dog, how did you train him?" Andy asked, staring the ugly man square in the eye. "Did you poke him and punch him? Is that why he's acting like this?"

"We didn't hurt him. We just did what we had to do to make him a good watchdog."

Zack's elbow flew out and jabbed Roy in the ribs. Roy sneered at him and rubbed his side.

"Ouch! What's that about?"

Before Zack could answer, the sheriff man leaned his arms on the fence and smiled at Roy.

"Well, that's strange. In the report you gave us, you said that you'd paid five hundred dollars to get this dog professionally trained. Now you're saying that you trained him. Is that right?"

"No . . . no. We paid to have him . . . uh . . . uh . . . trained," Roy stammered. "I'm talking about the follow-up stuff that they had us do. The trainer told us to do. Yeah, that's what I meant."

"I know quite a few dog trainers." Andy stood beside the sheriff man. His eyes tightened when he looked at Roy. "Who did you use?"

"Uh . . . I don't remember his name. Smith or something like that." Roy stepped back a little.

"If I had paid someone five hundred dollars, I would know his name for sure. You got a receipt or canceled check for that training?" The sheriff man pulled out a writing pad from his pocket.

The sound of another car came to my ears. I glanced up and saw Bethany pull into the driveway. There was a worried look on her face when she stepped out and came toward the backyard.

"I've had enough of this foolishness," Roy grumped. "We come to fetch our dog back to the dump. All you're supposed to do, Mr. Cop Man, is just see that we get it done and stay out of our way. Come on, Zack. Help me get Spike."

Roy flung the gate open and marched toward the doghouse.

Jake's tail stopped wagging. The hair on Ding's back bristled. I growled.

"What's going on?" Bethany called. Now she was jogging toward us instead of just walking. "Did something happen?"

No one answered her.

"Come here, Spikey Boy. Come on out." Zack looked into the doghouse.

"Get that mangy dog out of there." Roy kicked at the house. When Spike didn't move, he kicked at it again. "Dump it over, Zack. We'll get him, one way or the other."

"I think you boys better back off!" the sheriff man yelled.

Zack picked up the back side of the doghouse, and Spike slid toward the opening. I could hear his feet, frantically scraping on the wood floor. Roy grabbed Spike's leg and finished dragging him out.

"You'd better get over here, or I'll break your leg off, you mangy dog!" the man roared. He raised his fist and glared at Spike.

"Quit yelling at him." Bethany rushed up. "You're scaring the dogs." When her eyes saw his angry fist raised, she grabbed his arm. "Don't! Please don't hit him."

Roy pushed Bethany!

She staggered back. Slipped. And went *kerplop*, right on her bottom.

That was too much!

"Grrrr. Get away from Bethany!" I snapped. Jake and Ding were right behind me. I grabbed hold of Roy's pant leg, snarling and shaking my head so hard I almost knocked myself down.

Roy screamed.

"Get that dog off me. He bit me." Roy slapped me upside the head. The instant I let go, he sprinted for the gate. Zack was hot on his heels as Ding and Jake growled and snapped at them. Andy helped Bethany up off of the ground and dusted her bottom.

"Are you okay, hon?"

"I'm fine." She smiled.

Once safe outside the backyard, with the gate latched, Roy grabbed his leg and started hopping around. As soon as they closed the gate, Jake, Ding, and I started leaping and snarling and snapping at the fence. Spike stood by his overturned doghouse and wagged his tail. The sheriff man stood beside Andy and Bethany.

"Are you all right, ma'am?"

"I'm fine." She smiled again. "Just lost my balance. I'm not hurt."

He nodded, reached down, and gave Spike a friendly pat on the head, then marched to the fence. Roy was still hopping around, holding one leg up in the air.

"I'm going to sue. That dog tried to tear my leg off. I'll probably never be able to walk again. I'm going to sue! Let's go, Zack. Forget that mangy dog. I'm going to get a lawyer. That crazy white dog bit me!" Roy yelled.

Smiling, the sheriff man leaned over the fence. "Would you please pull up your pant leg, sir. I need to see the wound."

Roy stopped hopping around and put both feet on the ground.

"It's bad. It's real bad. I'll probably have to go to the hospital."

"Let me see it, sir," the sheriff man repeated his order.

Roy sneered at him. "No."

"Well, then, hop in my car and I'll drive you to the emergency room."

"No way."

The sheriff man only smiled and pulled the note pad from his pocket.

"Guess I'll need to add that to my report, too." He talked to himself as he wrote on his little pad. "Victim refused to show the injury and refused transportation to seek medical treatment." He looked up and his smile got even bigger. "Let's see . . . what else do I need to put in here. Oh, yeah. Trespassing. You entered the yard illegally and without permission. Destruction of private property. Assault and battery—"

"Assault and battery?" Roy yelped. "No such thing!"

The sheriff man's eyebrows arched. "You attacked the lady over there and knocked her down. I'm a witness."

"She grabbed my arm . . . and . . . and . . ."

"I saw the whole thing." The sheriff man grinned. Then his eyes narrowed as he glared at Roy. "She never touched you!"

"But . . . but . . ." Roy stammered. Reluctantly he reached down and pulled his pant leg up. There wasn't a mark on him.

"That dog didn't even touch you. Go on and leave these nice folks alone," the sheriff man said.

"But look what he did to my pants. First they ruin our guard dog, then they sic that vicious mutt on me. At least they ought to pay for my pants. The leg's all shredded up and . . ."

Zack grabbed Roy's arm and pulled him toward the black truck.

"There was no damage to your person," the sheriff man called after them. "As far as these people stealing your dog . . . I know these people . . . they wouldn't steal your dog. You may have a case if you can prove ownership and a receipt for training a dog. My hunch is that you don't have receipts. Any training your dog ever got came from being knocked around and beaten. Probably need to add animal abuse to this record. There *is* a law against that." The sheriff man stood straight and tall.

"We'll see," Roy remarked over his shoulder.

"My advice to you, sir, is to leave and never come back." The sheriff man *was not* smiling anymore. "This report will be kept in the file. If any of these animals turn up missing or hurt or sick, I'll personally come out to your junkyard and drag you in. Fact is, if these nice people so much as tell me they see your pickup driving down their road—I'm coming after you. Got it?"

Roy didn't answer. He did nod his head, though.

"Ah, come on, Zack. Let's get out of here." He growled, kind of leaning to the side to see past us and look at Spike. "That dog ain't no use to us, anyhow. Never was worth shooting. We'll just get us a better dog."

Roy stepped into the truck and slammed the door. Zack hurried around to get in on his side. Roy took off before he got there. Zack had to jump, open the door, and swing himself in as the truck was moving. Dirt and rocks flew everywhere as the truck roared away.

"Sorry, folks. Everyone in the sheriff's department—police department, too, for that matter—we all know Roy Ferguson. He's about as worthless as they come. Always threatening to sue someone or trying to get money out of them. But he did file a report, and we had to respond to it." The sheriff man walked back to the yard. "He won't bother you again. I'd bet money on it."

"We appreciate all of your help." Andy reached over the fence and shook his hand. "We certainly wouldn't steal anyone's dog!"

Jake, Ding, Spike, and I all ran to put our front paws on the fence. We licked his hand and thanked him, too.

"Good dogs you got." The young man smiled. "They're pretty good judges of character." He ruffled the hair on my head. "This one was going to tear Roy up." I licked his hand again.

With a laugh, he strolled back toward his car.

"Thanks again, Mr. Jones," Andy and Bethany both called as they waved at him.

When things calmed down, Bethany went

inside and fixed us all a special treat. Even Biff and Barkie got pancakes and syrup.

Ding was right. The stuff was yummy, but it did stick to the roof of my mouth.

"I can't believe that big white fluffy dog," Bethany said as she and Andy watched us eat. "He's always been the sweetest thing. Never even growls at the other dogs. I just couldn't believe he was going to tear that guy up."

"Well"—Andy shrugged—"when that man pushed you down, tearing him up was the same thought that crossed my mind. Your white dog just beat me to it."

"Guess we need to keep him around. He's a pretty good watchdog." Bethany petted my head.

Spike trotted up and Andy scratched behind his ears. Tail wagging so fast and hard that it stirred the air, he smiled at me.

"Thanks for helping me, Freddie," he yapped. "You're the best friend a dog could ever have. I love you."

It was good to have a home. Good to feel needed. Good to be loved.

ABOUT THE AUTHORS

Carol Wallace and Bill Wallace have always had lots of pets. Most are "strays" that they have taken in. And most—if not all—became characters in their books.

Mush (who goes by Freddie in this story, but used the name Snow in Bub Moose) is sweet— most of the time; clumsy—some of the time; and so lovable that she wormed her way into their hearts from the very first day she appeared at their home. She's lovable until . . . she finds something stinky to roll in.

April (Spike in the story) is also lovable— with family and friends. When someone unknown shows up . . . LOOK OUT! Just like the other five dogs in the family, she can be the meanest hound around.

Carol Wallace is the wife of award-winning author Bill Wallace. The couple resides in Chickasha, Oklahoma. Carol was an elementary school teacher. Both Bill and Carol hold master's degrees in elementary education from Southwestern Oklahoma State University.